SARAH M. ANDERSON WRITING AS

MAGGIE CHASE

HIS
SAPPHIRE

Acknowledgements

I could not have written this book without the generous help of the following people: Melissa Jolly for everything she does, Shae O'Conner and Laura K. Curtis for their support, Tasha Harrison and Mary Dieterich for editing, and Alexandra Haughton for designing the cover.

Dedication

To Tiffany Reisz and CJ Lemire

Chapter One

Judge Gerard Hobson stood in his office, looking out the narrow window that faced Main Street.

He couldn't remember the last time he'd slept. Two days ago? Maybe three. His eyes felt like someone had ground sand into them and his jaw wasn't much better. Everything about him was scratchy and irritable.

He'd lost the election for mayor of Brimstone, Texas—again. That in and of itself grated, but in the months since the election, he'd forged ahead. There were other ways to assume power, after all. But then that upstart whelp of Isabelle's, Raymond Dupree, had been chosen as the representative for the constitutional convention in Austin, Texas. Gerard had convinced himself that losing the election wouldn't be that bad, if he got appointed to the convention.

But he hadn't even gotten that.

Where had he gone wrong? He was doing the right thing. He *always* did the right thing. He'd attempted to impose order upon this lawless town of Brimstone. This was *his* town, for God's sake. His grandfather, a hellfire-and-damnation preacher, had founded this town ten miles away from Fort Adams to save the God-fearing people from the sins of soldiers.

1

But did that matter? No. Brimstone had willingly settled into degeneracy and rebuffed every single one of Gerard's efforts to lead them back towards a righteous path.

Why wouldn't people do what he told them to? His actions were moral. The law was on his side. He was a God-fearing man. People should have been begging for him to take control of this town and set it on the correct path.

But were they? No. Instead, at every available opportunity to make the righteous choice, the people of this hellhole repeatedly chose that sinner, Raymond Dupree. They chose the brothels and the saloons over the path of moral righteousness. They chose sin and violence.

Just like Isabelle had chosen Leopold Dupree all those years ago. All because Gerard had made a mistake and shown her what he really was. The last mistake he'd made.

Or so he'd thought.

Now this. He glanced back at the newspaper on his desk. It was a vile broadsheet—normally filled with murderers and crime and innuendo. But today took the cake.

"Judge Hobson rumored to be suspect in whore's disappearance."

No doubt, this was the work of his enemies. Dupree's man, Hank O'Shea—he was probably behind this ridiculously fabricated story. Wasn't it bad enough that Dupree was a living reminder of his failures? That Dupree beat him every time they came up against each other in an election? Did the impudent pup have to completely ruin Gerard's reputation?

The darkness within Gerard rose up and this time, he felt powerless to hold it at bay. His fingers clenched into fists and he struggled to hang onto his control. But he was failing. He just wanted to hit someone. He'd spent years mastering his darkness—years of living by a strict moral code that kept him far from sin—and where had it gotten him?

"Judge Hobson rumored to be suspect in whore's disappearance."

The article was full of unsubstantiated innuendo. Four years ago, a prostitute from Beantown—over thirty miles north of Brimstone—had been dumped a few miles outside of town, her body cut to ribbons. The story said she was found with a silk necktie in her mouth and had made libelous claims that it was the same kind of necktie that he wore.

The darkness in him—it could have done that to a girl. That was why he had to keep it under control.

He hadn't killed that girl. Hell, he hadn't even been near a woman in years. Decades. Not since Isabelle. It was too risky.

He despised Raymond Dupree and his man, Hank O'Shea—but they were right about Gerard. He was dangerous. He always had been. He'd recognized that early.

He scrubbed a hand over his face. He was so, *so* tired. Tired of telling people what they should be doing and tired of them ignoring him. He was tired of losing to Dupree and tired of playing this cat and mouse game with O'Shea.

"Titus!" he called out.

Titus stuck his bull head through the office door. "Yes, Judge?"

3

For one brief second, Gerard mourned the fact that he hadn't been able to move Hank O'Shea away from Dupree. Titus served a purpose, but he didn't have any brains to speak of. Gerard appreciated that the man did what he was told, when he was told to do it, but he would never be anything more than a blunt instrument. "I need you to bring someone to me."

He couldn't push back against the darkness. Not anymore.

"An arrest?" Titus fancied himself a deputy.

Gerard shook his head. This would be outside of the law.

Titus's face sank into disappointment, rather like a hound dog that was kept on a leash. "Who?"

Gerard turned his attention back out to the narrow window. He was going to burn in hell for this. "Bring me Mistress."

*

"Sapphire?"

Sadie sat up straighter. The man who had his hand underneath her skirt didn't pull it away. Of course he didn't. In the saloon of the Jeweled Ladies, men were allowed to touch the whores like this— encouraged, even. It helped make the sale—get a man so worked up that he was only too happy to pay over four times what a dove at one of the other whorehouses in town charged.

Sadie stared up at Mistress, her whole body quivering with anticipation. She knew that tone of voice and it usually came with a 'special request.' She hadn't had a special request in quite some time now

4

and she was tired of playing around with men in the saloon who thought they knew how to give a woman what she wanted—men like Mr. Miller. In reality, none of them did. "Yes, Mistress?"

"I am so sorry, Mr. Miller, but I require Sapphire's assistance at this time." Mistress waved a hand and Garnet came forward. "Garnet will be happy to entertain you in Sapphire's absence."

Mr. Miller started to protest as Sadie slipped away from his diddling fingers. But before he could complain too much, Garnet molded herself to his lap and threaded her hands through his greasy hair as if she'd been waiting all night for this opportunity.

It was then that Sadie noticed the man standing in the doorway of the saloon. He was a giant ox of a man, with narrow, dull eyes and no noticeable neck to speak of. He was just a head perched on shoulders. She had the distinct impression that he was not terribly bright.

"Mistress…" She asked hesitantly as Mistress led her back toward the ox. This wouldn't be the man Mistress was going to give her to, would it? Any pain that he would inflict would be blunt, the kind that snapped bones. Although some people believed that pain was pain, Sapphire had a different opinion. She much preferred her bones unbroken, thank you.

And as Mistress paid her good money to take pain, Sadie's opinion was the only one that mattered, wasn't it?

For Sadie craved the release of pain. She needed it as she needed air to breathe and water to drink. But there were so few men in this town who understood the rules of the game. She did not want to be beaten to a pulp or ripped to shreds. She did not want to be abused. Used, perhaps. There was a place and a time for that.

The gentleman—if she could call him—who was waiting for her and Mistress did not look like a man who understood the game. He looked like someone who wanted a punching bag.

Mistress must have sensed her hesitation, because she threaded her arm through Sadie's and led her on. "I have to make a... special trip," Mistress said, her voice tight with tension even as she tried to hide it with a light laugh. "I would like you to accompany me." She said it in a tone of voice that made it clear that it was not truly a request.

This was unusual. The Mistress of the Jeweled Ladies had a specific set of rules that she adhered to above all others and one of those rules was that her Jewels were not allowed to entertain men away from the brothel. There was safety in numbers and that way Mistress could keep an eye on her girls.

They reached the hall, where the man waited. His mouth hung slightly open and for all the world, he looked like a cow chewing its cud.

Please, let it not be him. Because her services were so very specialized, Sadie had significantly more say in whom she allowed to pay for her time. She knew her limits and she knew how to keep herself safe and she would absolutely not put herself in a closed room with someone who did not respect either of those two things.

"Mr. Titus, I am ready." Mistress sounded imperial with this statement.

Mr. Titus blinked at her and looked at Sadie. "I'm only supposed to bring you," he said, sounding just as dumb as he looked. Perhaps dumber.

Mistress gave Sadie's arm a little squeeze. "Oh, but I insist. I'm sure it will be just fine." She leaned forward and patted the giant man on the cheek. "I won't let you get in trouble," she added, in what was probably supposed to be a motherly voice that didn't quite make it.

Sadie kept her face pleasant and blank through this entire exchange. So Mr. Titus was not the man making the special request—that was a relief. But that didn't answer any question. Who was requesting Mistress's presence? Why were they doing so at a time when the Jeweled Ladies was busy? And why was Mistress bringing her along?

"He won't like it," Mr. Titus said, but even Sadie could hear that he'd already given up.

They paused at the entryway where Samuel, the big colored doorman, was looking anxious. "Samuel," Mistress said in a businesslike tone, "please keep an eye on the establishment while I'm gone. I shan't be long."

The weather was still quite warm for November, which was good considering that Sadie had not had the chance to grab a cloak or even a scarf. At least she still had on her long opera gloves, she thought as she and Mistress strolled down the sidewalk arm in arm behind Mr. Titus. Mistress kept her head up and her shoulders back, a genial smile on her face. Sadie took her cues and did the same. They were not being summoned by some mysterious stranger. They were out for a stroll together, enjoying a lovely evening.

Sadie was more than a little surprised, however, when Mr. Titus turned first down an alley and then into the back of the courthouse before leading the women upstairs. He knocked on the door and waited until a voice said, "Enter."

Mr. Titus opened the door and there sat Judge Hobson, his head bent over his work. Sadie began to worry in earnest. Was Mistress under arrest? What *was* this?

"The ladies are here," Mr. Titus said. He made a motion as if he were going to shove Mistress and Sadie into the room, but Mistress neatly sidestepped him and pulled Sadie along after her.

"Thank you, Mr. Titus," she said in that haughty voice again. "You may go. And please close the door behind you. That's a good boy."

Sadie had to hide her smile behind her hand. Mistress was treating Mr. Titus like he was a lapdog.

Hobson had not looked up before this moment, but when he did, he focused directly on Sadie. A chill passed over her as his gaze bore into her. It took all of her self-control not to shiver, but she had prodigious control over her body and its reactions.

"Who is she?" he sneered.

"I promised Mr. Titus you would not be mad at him when I insisted upon bringing Miss Sapphire Bleu along with me." Mistress released her arm and gracefully lowered herself into one of the two chairs before the judge's desk. Clearly, the judge did not intimidate the woman. Sadie couldn't say the same thing.

She knew who he was, of course. Everyone in this town knew who Judge Gerard Hobson was. He ruled from his bench like a king from on high. He was moral and righteous and upstanding and he detested—*detested*—anything that reeked of sin and impropriety.

And there were few things that he detested more than the Jeweled Ladies or Mistress. Closing down the brothels and regulating the saloons was one of the key things he'd campaigned on.

If Sadie could've voted, she would've voted against him.

Thankfully, Judge Hobson had lost. While publicly, Mayor Raymond Dupree was not an advocate for the brothels, he'd married one of Mistress's finest Jewels, Miss Emerald Green—now Mrs. Emmeline Dupree. That connection had afforded a certain measure of security about the status of the Jeweled Ladies within the town of Brimstone.

"This conversation is meant for your ears only, madam," Judge Hobson said in a chillingly cold voice. "If I wanted a whore, I would've asked for one."

Mistress left this statement hanging in the air for a moment. Then, without replying directly, she said, "Sapphire, darling, do take a seat."

Hobson fixed her with a hard glare and although she wanted to do as Mistress said, she found she couldn't. This was his office and his chair. She stood until he sighed and said, "Sit."

She kept her movements smooth and fluid as she stepped forward and sank into the other chair. She expected Mistress to be put out with her, but instead the older woman turned and gave her a pleased little smile.

Hobson glared at her and then at Mistress. For the first time, Sadie noticed that his eyes were red with dark circles underneath. And he hadn't shaved in a day or two. He looked haggard and worn. If any other man had looked like that, she would be tempted to feel sorry for them, but not Hobson. He'd done everything in his power to destroy the Jeweled Ladies and Mistress—and especially Emerald Green. Sadie refused to extend even the slightest hint of pity to this man. But even considering the fact that he looked terrible, the man was quite handsome. He was considerably older—possibly even older than Mistress herself, although no one knew how old she was. Probably in his fifties, Sadie would guess. His hair had gone a silvery shade of gray and even in his current state, his jacket was pressed and his necktie as fresh looking as if he'd tied it ten minutes ago. Yes, everything he wore was black, except for the crisp linen shirt, but there was a certain sartorial *panache* to the man.

She said nothing because she had no idea why she or Mistress were here. Being silent in a situation such as this was no hardship. However, neither Mistress nor Hobson seemed inclined to jump into the gap. The silence in the room stretched until it felt like something was going to break.

Well, one thing was clear. The judge and Mistress were locked in a rather fierce battle of the wills. But then again, that was old news.

The judge broke first, his voice gravelly with displeasure. Sadie snapped to attention when he spoke. "The next time I make a request of you, Mistress, I expect you to fulfill it. Or are you not paid to do what men tell you to?"

If Mistress was offended, she didn't show it. Instead, she gave the judge a sly little smile that seemed to say that she had the man right where she wanted him. "Of course I am, your honor. But, as of right now, you haven't paid me anything so…" She gave a delicate little shrug. "If you're looking to change that situation, of course I will become more amendable to your every wish."

"I do not pay for sex, madam. The very thought is repugnant."

Again, it wasn't like that statement was a surprise. However, it did seem a little more shocking considering to whom he was saying it, Sadie thought.

Mistress tilted her head to the side as she took in his haggard appearance. "In my world," she began in a tone that was almost diplomatic instead of teasing, "I have found that people pay for many things. Sex is just a convenient catchall. Wouldn't you agree, Miss Bleu?"

Sadie couldn't keep the smile off of her face. For certain select clientele, sex was the last thing they paid her for. "Oh, I quite agree, Mistress." She looked at the judge to gauge his reaction to this.

He was staring at the top of his desk—no, Sadie realized, not at the desk. The newspaper on top of it. She leaned forward and barely caught the headline. *Oh.* Suddenly it all made sense.

The article. That one that had all but accused him of murdering a prostitute some years ago. They'd all read the article at the Jeweled Ladies, of course—what poetic justice, it seemed, that the most moral man in Brimstone could be brought so low by his own peccadilloes.

"Was this your doing?" He sounded so bleak.

"My dear Judge Hobson," Mistress said with an obvious edge in her voice, "if I were going to destroy you, doing so in the press would be the final blow, not the opening salvo. Besides," she went on, as if she hadn't just threatened an officer of the law, "I happen to believe you're innocent. Capable of violence, but innocent in this particular situation."

Hobson sat back, clearly stunned by this judgment. "You do?"

"You do?" Sadie echoed. This would be the perfect way to get Hobson out of their lives forever. Even the hint of scandal would taint his judgments from here on out and he would have no political clout to threaten the brothels or the saloons. Why would Mistress give him an out?

Mistress turned her attention to Sadie. "Know your enemy, dear. The honorable judge and I have been dancing around each other for a long time now. If he were to make use of any brothel within a two-day ride of Brimstone, I would know."

"You have me followed?" he asked in disgust, pushing away from the desk and standing. He turned his back on the two women and stared at a narrow window.

"Of course not. I have better things to do than shadow your every move. But it only makes good business sense to maintain close ties with my fellow madams in all the local whorehouses. They know they can appeal to me for aid if needed and in return, they keep me informed of certain things. They all know who you are and what you look like. But more than that, they all know *what* you're looking for."

Sadie saw the tension ripple down the judge's back at this final statement. "Ridiculous, madam. I look for nothing that you could offer me."

"And yet, here we are."

When the judge didn't say anything, Sadie decided it was time to enter the conversation. "Why are we here?" Because she'd been pulled away from a paying customer to come watch Mistress and Judge Hobson snipe at each other. It was entertaining, but it would not add to her bank account.

"I'm so glad you asked, Miss Bleu," Mistress replied with a wink. "We're here for one very simple reason."

"And that is?" Sadie asked after a pause—a pause that was not filled by the judge. He seemed intent on ignoring them, which was rude considering he'd asked them to be here.

That was stretching it, she knew. He hadn't asked for her to be here. But Mistress had brought her anyway and now she was a part of this—whatever *this* was.

"We're here because the Honorable Judge Hobson is surrendering."

Sadie's gaze flew to the judge. She expected him to deny this—to loudly proclaim that Mistress had lost her mind. Heavens, Sadie wouldn't be surprised if the judge had them arrested. It had happened before.

He did none of those things. Instead, he seemed to draw into himself. His head dropped and his shoulders rounded. He very much looked like a man who was giving up.

"To what is he surrendering?" she asked carefully because it didn't seem that he was on the verge of resigning and no one had made any mention of him moving to a new town.

"An excellent question, dear. Judge Hobson? Care to answer that question?"

13

He sighed, but made no move to reply.

"To his demons, of course. Oh, he tries so hard." Mistress leaned over and rested a hand on Sadie's arm, tapping with one of her fingers. "He tries so very hard not to have any demons. But you and I know that all men do."

Sadie studied the judge again. He made no move to correct Mistress.

Slowly, she began to see where this was going—why she was here. She played along because in this situation because making a false assumption could be hazardous to her health. "And what sort of demons does a man like Judge Hobson have?"

Mistress glanced at the silent man, but he was still just that—silent. After a respectable moment, she went on, "Demons he fears, dear. A man like Judge Hobson values control above everything else. And right now, he has lost that control. Lost all semblance of it. The town will not bow to his wishes. *I* will not bow to his wishes. And Mayor Dupree continues to confound him."

This was a language that Sadie understood.

This was why she was here.

Mistress nodded in acknowledgment. "Yes. If he has already lost control, how can he possibly expect to fight against those demons?"

"He can't," Sadie whispered. "He can't deny his true self when everything else has been stripped away." Just saying the words aloud sent a thrill through her.

To be stripped bare, given no place to hide? Forced to face the craven nature of your desires? Giving in to those needs and coming out on the other

14

side stronger and better? That was what she lived for. Sadly, it was also a rare thing. But that just made the few occasions when she dealt with the proper man all the more special.

"You understand perfectly, my dear. But this does leave the judge with a problem," Mistress went on in the diplomatic tone of hers. "The judge is lost. He has had such an iron grip on his control for so long that he has no idea how to proceed. He cannot and will not patronize establishments such as the Jeweled Ladies. If he could, I would already know about it. Instead, he has lived a clean, sober life for so long that now..." She shrugged again. "He is lost in the darkness and he cannot see his way back to the light."

Control. Judge Hobson was a man who needed it. Thrived on it. But he'd made a judgment in error for he'd tried to impose his will upon people who did not consent to submit.

But she did. "How shall we help him, then? For I admit, I hold no great love for the judge, but it pains me to see a man suffer so."

Mistress laughed, a delicate, tinkling noise. "Love so rarely figures into this, doesn't it? The answer is obvious. We give him something to control." She tilted her head, a knowing smile on her lips. "Or rather, *someone*. Someone who will take his word as law, who will take the cruelty he fears and embrace it. Someone who will surrender to him, unconditionally." She arched an eyebrow and Sadie beamed. "Someone rather like you, Miss Bleu."

This all sounded well and good coming from Mistress's lips—but what of the judge? Sadie looked at the man. He was now leaning on the sill, looking as if he'd been horsewhipped. He hadn't said a single thing the entire time she and Mistress had been talking. His silence spoke quite loudly.

"I don't know," Sadie said truthfully. "I wouldn't want to put anyone at risk. And we have rules," she reminded Mistress. "I don't believe the judge would delight in being seen entering our place and I would not wish to meet him alone in his office or in his home. Control is such a delicate thing—I've seen what can happen when it snaps. Perhaps he fears his darkness with good reason."

"Yes," Mistress sighed sympathetically, her gaze fastened on the newspaper on Hobson's desk. "It can be such a sad thing when done poorly." Suddenly, she stood. "I'm sure you're quite right, Miss Bleu. There is nothing that we can do for the judge. So it would be best for us to take our leave."

Sadie blinked up at her. That was *it*? They were leaving? But then, the judge hadn't turned around. He hadn't even acknowledged that they were there after a certain point.

Mistress moved toward the door. "Come along, Sapphire." She swept out of the room as grandly as any queen.

Resigned, Sadie stood and smoothed her skirts. She heard Mistress talking to Mr. Titus, reassuring him that he was not in trouble for bringing two ladies instead of one.

She paused in the doorway, her hand on the knob, and looked back at Judge Hobson. She did pity him, just a little bit. She saw the situation quite clearly now. He would not allow himself what he wanted and therefore, he would not allow anyone else to have

16

what they wanted, either. What a lonely way to live, controlled by the one thing he sought to master.

She hesitated and then spoke. "Surrender," she told him, "can be freeing." He shuddered, so she knew he'd heard her. It gave her the courage to go on, "It can be your salvation."

He didn't respond. But then, what had she expected?

Sadie closed the door behind her.

Chapter Two

They were almost back to the Jeweled Ladies before Mistress spoke. "Thank you for accompanying me, Sapphire."

"My pleasure, Mistress. It was... enlightening." The judge was not only subject to the same needs as other men, but he'd been brought low by them. *Enlightening*, indeed. "Do you think we shall see him again?" Because for all of Mistress's talk about surrender, the man had said and done exactly nothing that indicated that he was giving into his dark needs—anything beyond speaking face-to-face with Mistress, that was.

Mistress mulled this question over until they were safely inside the Jeweled Ladies. "I believe we shall," she said, leading Sadie not to the parlor or the saloon, but upstairs to her office.

This time, when Mistress motioned to the chair in front of the desk, Sadie sat without hesitation. "Do you think we can trust him?" Because her services were founded on trust. And misplacing that trust—well, that was how whores wound up dead.

Mistress sat also, lost in thought. "We will have to be careful."

"I'm always careful, Mistress."

18

Mistress shook her head. "Do you remember when I found you? You were not careful at all, my dear girl. You were a wild slip of a girl prowling through the most dangerous of dockside saloons, all but asking people to rape you." She paused. "Not to mention the warrant out for your arrest."

Sadie knew she should be embarrassed by her history, but she hadn't been able to stop herself. The danger had been intoxicating.

She shuddered. She knew few would view her actions as sane. She'd had a perfectly good marriage proposal from a perfectly fine man looking for a perfectly fine wife—his second. But all he'd spoken of when she'd enquired about their lives together after the marriage was how he would guard her and treasure her and it had all been meant to sound romantic and instead it had just sounded...

Dull. She'd known that suitor would never be able to satisfy her need for danger. So she'd stolen five hundred dollars from him and, when that ran out—because it had, all too quickly—she'd headed to the docks. It had scared the holy hell out of her and she'd loved every moment of it.

She missed that danger. She was far safer here—alive and whole and healthy, not to mention well-paid—but the flash of true fear...

She missed that.

Mistress interrupted her thoughts. "We will hear from Judge Hobson again. Are you willing to see him?"

Sadie thought back to the way he'd gripped the windowsill, how he'd commanded her to sit.

Mistress misunderstood her silence. "Don't fret, my dear. He will pay double."

Sadie gaped at her. "You think he'll pay thirty dollars for an hour?" She already earned fifteen dollars an hour for each special request, whereas most girls commanded no more than ten dollars—minus Mistress's cut, of course. Most run-of-the-mill visits earned a Jewel five dollars when a man wanted to be sucked off. Which added up quickly, but still…

Thirty dollars an hour was a fortune.

Mistress smiled that sly smile again. "My dear, I don't think he'll be paying by the hour. I imagine he'll pay upwards of a hundred dollars a session." Sadie's mouth dropped open and she stared in shock at Mistress. "He's paying for us to keep his secrets and that, to him, is nearly priceless."

"We… we aren't going to blackmail him, are we? I don't…" she shifted uncomfortably. Whoring was not exactly legal—but what she did was grounded in trust and extortion was a violation of that.

"No, no—of course not." Mistress waved this concern away. "He's a customer, just as any other man in this town is." She leaned back and looked Sadie up and down. "He will have to be taught, that is all. I doubt he has any idea what he's capable of or how to control himself—and I'm certain he has no idea how to play the game. He will pay—me, for the lessons and you, for compliance."

"You?" It was rare for Mistress to do anything in bed anymore.

Mistress had been Sadie's first true teacher. The older woman wasn't lying—Sadie had been wild when Mistress had found her. She'd been chasing pain and fear and should have been dead already—just like that whore who'd been cut up.

20

Mistress had plucked her out of the docks and carried her to Brimstone. She'd taught Sadie the rules of submission and domination, of sadism. She'd made Sadie into a lady—well paid, cultured and able to take far more than that wild girl had dreamed. Mistress had pushed Sadie into places that she'd only dreamed of down on those docks.

When Mistress smiled this time, there was real warmth. "My dear, I wouldn't entrust your safety to anyone else. *I* will train him. This will ensure everyone's safety. He cannot accuse me of spying if I'm in the room. You will be protected if there is a problem. And I…" she got a far-away look in her eyes before she straightened. "I will get to know our judge better. Unless…" Mistress added, studying her.

"Unless, Mistress?"

"Unless you refuse him. You are well within your rights to do so. You always have a choice—you, more than anyone else here."

Sadie dropped her gaze to her hands, which were twisting into the silk of her gown. Men who came to her for this—they had their needs, just as Mistress had told the judge. Sadie needed to please them, needed to let the pain push her into a place where nothing could touch her.

But this? The judge was different. Mistress had talked about surrender, but the judge hadn't given up. Not entirely. He was unpredictable—a rare quality, in a man. And that made him dangerous.

"The money will be quite good," Mistress said sympathetically. "Your sisters…"

Sadie looked at her in surprise. It was unusual for Mistress to acknowledge that her Jewels had a life outside of the brothel.

Sadie had six sisters, all younger. She'd found an aunt to take care of the little ones, but the woman had been destitute. The older ones went to finishing school now, learning how to be self-sufficient women. May, the one closest in age to Sadie, would find work as a schoolteacher or a governess soon. They wouldn't have to rely on anyone to survive. Not anymore. Not even Sadie. But that left the youngest ones still with Aunt Ethel. Aunt Ethel cared for the children, but no one else could pay the many bills that many small mouths incurred. It was all up to Sadie. Just like it had always been.

"I'm sure," she agreed.

Mistress opened her mouth, hesitated, and then spoke. "Sadie," she said gently, and Sadie started to hear her real name.

"Yes, Mistress?"

"You know, most girls have plans." Mistress was back to her diplomatic tone of voice. "They save their money and envision a life beyond these walls. Even Emerald—whom I thought would take over the business from me—she married and left this life behind."

Sadie nodded. Several girls had recently left and with each departure, she'd felt another stab of loneliness. She missed Abigail—Ebony White—most fiercely.

"But not you," Mistress went on, studying her intently now. "You've not spoken of plans or hopes. Don't you dream of marriage, a family? Or, like Ebony, a business?"

The question unexpectedly saddened her. For once, she'd made the grave mistake of falling in love with one of her regulars. For three months, Jonathan had come to visit her once a week. It hadn't taken long to realize that he was a skilled master. He'd taught her almost as much as Mistress had in those few visits.

Plus, Jonathan had been all of thirty-one, young and handsome with a mop of golden blond curls. He'd had an easy smile and a quick wit and he'd effortlessly brought Sadie to a crashing climax after each session in that attic room. That alone would have been enough to enthrall her, but it was what came after—the way he'd tenderly cared for her and then pulled her onto his lap, cuddling and kissing her and making sure she was well and happy.

Was it any wonder that she'd dreamed of a life with him?

And then, as quickly as it had started, it had ended. He'd shown up one final time to tell her it was over and give her a gift. Sadie had begged to go with him. *Begged.* And he'd responded…

"I am not the kind of woman men marry," she said, echoing Jonathan's cruel comments when he told her he'd found a proper bride. "Men want a mother. Children. I've raised enough." Six sisters was enough for anyone. She shook her head.

After Jonathan had left her, she held those dreams of marriage close to her heart, where they could not escape and wreak havoc on her life. Because in marriage she knew that she would have to deny her needs. She could not have both a husband and respectability and *also* have her wrists bound and her back flogged. Those were separate worlds and they would never cross. She'd always known it, too. Wasn't that why she'd given her sisters over to Aunt Ethel and started working the docks? Because she could not be a schoolmarm or a governess and no one would marry a woman who didn't want to raise another baby. No one. "There is no other place for me in the world."

Mistress let this statement hang. "Even now," she murmured when Sadie began to fidget, "you do not look toward the future? You could ask to be trained as my replacement, you know."

"I enjoy pain, Mistress. I do not enjoy disappointment. We both know I do not have the temperament to run this business. Not like you do. I would be a poor mistress."

Mistress inclined her head in acknowledgement of this simple fact. "You are already a woman of means," Mistress said, turning her attention to some papers on her desk. "The judge can make you a wealthy woman. Perhaps you should think beyond tomorrow or the next day."

Sadie heard the dismissal in her voice. She stood. "Yes, Mistress." She turned, mentally preparing herself for another evening in the saloon, with men taking their pleasure from her without offering any in exchange.

She needed something more—especially after the confusion of this evening. She didn't want to think about what she wanted or what she should do to get it—she wanted someone to tell her what to do. She wanted the freedom of surrender, tonight more than she had in quite some time.

Sadie paused at the door, tempted to ask Mistress to take her up to the attic and take over. It had been a long time since Mistress had grabbed her by her hair, thrown her down and stood over her with a riding crop. Pearl would do it, too—but Sadie preferred Mistress. Pearl was too cold by half and her style of cruelty was more mental than physical. That wasn't how Sadie liked to submit.

But when she turned back, she found Mistress staring at her, her eyes knowing. "Soon," the older woman said with a smile. "The judge will be here soon, I predict. And anticipation is very… challenging, is it not? Until then," she went on, "I trust you'll keep this strictly between us." It was not a question.

"Of course, Mistress."

Sadie left, wondering exactly how long she'd have to wait for release.

And whether or not Judge Gerard Hobson would be worth that wait.

*

Surrender, it turned out, was not as simple as Gerard had envisioned.

For the next three days, he attempted to forget the conversation with Mistress and that young whore, Sapphire Bleu. He'd never heard a name so damned ridiculous as Sapphire Bleu. And, as was apparently Mistress's custom, the young woman had been attired head-to-toe in a rich blue color—all except the white gloves that had covered most of her otherwise bare arms.

Really. The nerve of that woman, bringing that girl along to what should have been a private conversation. It was more sand in the wound, another layer of irritation that only got maddeningly worse because, with that girl sitting right there, Gerard hadn't been able to even broach the topic of…

25

Of paying for a woman.

But a woman to do what? To have sex with him, just like she did with everyone else who flipped her two bits?

No. He wasn't going to lie to himself. Not anymore.

He'd wanted a woman to punish. He'd had Mistress brought to him because he wanted to punish *her*. Legally, he couldn't. He could have her arrested and brought to trial, but public opinion would never be in his favor. She held too many men in her pockets. Including their illustrious mayor.

But privately...

And instead, that infuriating woman had brought that girl. *Sapphire.*

The one who had stood there, looking at him with huge blue eyes, until he'd given her permission to sit.

The one who had not run screaming in horror when Mistress had suggested that Gerard take his cruelty out on someone just like her.

The one who had paused when they had a scant few seconds alone together and had told him that surrender could be *his* salvation.

He was beyond saving. And after three days of struggling to hold himself together, he finally admitted it. He composed a letter.

Mistress, join me in my chambers Wednesday evening. Bring the girl.

He sent the note off with Titus and then tried to turn his attention back to his work. He suspected that Mistress would ignore his letter for as long as possible.

Therefore, he was surprised when the reply came within a quarter of an hour.

Your Honor, it is with regret that I refuse. Any such further meetings must be conducted in the safety of the Jeweled Ladies.

Gerard scowled at the note before dashing off a reply.

Unacceptable. I cannot be seen going in or out of your house of ill repute. Bring the girl to me.

Another quarter of an hour passed before, panting, Titus reappeared with the response.

Good sir, I will do no such thing. Miss Bleu has consented to see you again, but any such meeting must be made on our terms, for our protection. Should you wish to enjoy what she has to offer you—and you do— you will come to the back door of the Jeweled Ladies at seven Saturday morning. Wear a different coat and a hat or otherwise disguise your appearance. You will wait in the room I will set aside for you until the rest of the girls have left to do their shopping. Then, and only then, will you and Miss Bleu have a chance to discuss your mutual, shared desires.

Was that whore seriously telling him what to do? He was desperate but not that damn desperate. Was he?

No. He was not. Gerard almost crumpled the note and threw it away. But then he saw the postscript.

P.S. I will do everything within my power to protect you. I promise you exactly nothing more and nothing less. The rest is up to you.

She was lying. She had to be. She didn't care for him. She'd dance a jig if he were so disgraced he had to leave town. They all would.

His hands were shaking and the note had gotten torn, somehow. But in the midst of his anger, Miss

27

Bleu's face floated before his vision. She should've been afraid of him. He was terrifying. He scared himself, the urges he had. If she'd had a brain in her head, she should've run screaming, just like Isabelle had.

But she hadn't. She'd left reluctantly, almost. She'd spoken softly to him. She'd spoken of more than just salvation and surrender. She'd spoken of rules and control.

At no point had she been scared of him.

In the end, of course he surrendered. Complete and total surrender. He bowed to Mistress's wishes, which only made his self-loathing that much more difficult to swallow.

Fine. I will be there. But if this is a trick, I will bury you, madam.

He got no response. But then, he hadn't expected one.

Chapter Three

Disguised as a laborer—stained work shirt, stained work pants, muddy shoes, no jacket and his normal top hat safely in his wardrobe at home, replaced with a slouch hat worn low over his eyes— Gerard moved unnoticed through the streets of Brimstone. He hunched over to disguise his height and shuffled his feet instead of walking with his normal long strides. It was lowering, to be seen like this. The only relief was that, by and large, no one seemed to take notice of him.

As a concession to his vanity, he carried a box with his regular clothes in it. The box was designed to look like something that might contain turnips or something, complete with bits of straw sticking out of the lid. But inside were his proper clothes. He may need to be invisible going into the Jeweled Ladies but he did not wish to sit across from either Mistress or Miss Bleu smelling of mud—or worse.

At promptly seven in the morning, he knocked on the kitchen door of the brothel. It was shoved open by a wide black woman with a clean white cloth tied around her head. "Is that Mistress's special order?" she said in a thick southern accent, waving him in.

Gerard didn't speak. He just nodded.

"Wait here." The black woman disappeared through a wide swinging door.

Gerard looked around. The kitchen was a large room, spotless and well appointed. Copper pots hung over a massive stove and a hearth built into the wall already had bread baking in it. In short, it didn't look like a den of sin. It looked like the kitchen one might expect in a fine hotel.

The swinging door burst open and the black woman barged back into the kitchen. Gerard jumped. Mistress breezed into the kitchen after the black woman, looking as fresh and perfectly put together as Gerard had ever seen her. Did she not sleep?

"Ah, yes," she said when she looked Gerard in the face. "Bring that this way, please."

The cook didn't so much as spare Gerard another glance as he followed Mistress out of the kitchen and into the Jeweled Ladies.

Much like the kitchen, the place was not what he was expecting. Of course, that might have been because dawn was still struggling to break through the early winter darkness. But the house was nearly silent as he followed Mistress upstairs. The house was far larger than it looked from the outside and there was no sign of impropriety. No stockings or corsets flung about haphazardly, no drunks sleeping it off in the stairwell. The hall had a light, pleasant smell of lemons and the doors to all the rooms they passed were closed.

Gerard felt a little of his tension fade. The walls were papered with a delicate floral pattern and the carpeting that muffled their footfalls looked Persian. The whole effect was pleasing—tasteful, even. As was the mirrored hat stand at one end of the hallway. This was… not so bad. If that were possible.

They mounted another set of stairs that led to another hallway that was nearly identical to the one on the second floor. And still, he might have been in one of the finest hotels instead of a notorious brothel.

Then Mistress produced a key from somewhere and opened a small door tucked into the end of the hall. They continued up. The tasteful wallpaper gave way to whitewash and the rug became rag. But the stairs made no noise as she led him up.

It was only when they'd achieved the top of the stairs and she unlocked another door that Gerard found his voice. "What is this?"

Mistress cut him a sharp look, but didn't answer. Instead, she motioned him through the door and shut it behind her. "This," she said, tucking the key back into her bodice, "is where you and Miss Bleu shall meet. I shall supervise, of course."

Gerard didn't like that. "I don't need an audience."

Her eyes narrowed sharply. "You do, however, need instruction. Have you ever acted upon your desires? Your demons, as you call them?" Gerard scowled at her. "I thought not. Miss Bleu is special to me, sir. I would not see her harmed by someone who doesn't know what he is doing."

He looked around. The room he found himself in was surprisingly sumptuous. The walls were covered with tapestries and a plush rug—perhaps Persian, but far thicker looking. The room had a hushed quality to it. He couldn't hear anything from the street. "And I'm to wait here on your attendance for hours?"

She nodded her head and then motioned to the

31

box in his arms. "I hope you brought something to read?"

He gave her a dull look. "I brought my real clothes."

"Quite right." He didn't like that sly smile on her face. "Well, I'll leave you. If you don't mind, I'll lock the door behind me. I wouldn't want anyone accidentally stumbling upon you. Only Miss Bleu and I have the key."

His first reaction was *absolutely not*. He would not be caged like a criminal, no matter how luxurious this room was.

But if they were the only people who had a key... "Leave your key with me."

She shook her head, somehow managing to look regretful. "Alas, I also cannot risk you wandering the halls. The girls are off duty, so to speak. A man in the house right now—no matter the state of his dress— would cause alarm."

He scowled again, harder this time. But he'd come this far. "I don't have to like it."

"No, I expect giving up this measure of control grates." Was it his imagination or did she sound... sympathetic? "Please make yourself comfortable." She motioned to a washstand, where he saw fresh water in the bowl. "Don't worry—no one below will hear you." Her grin turned sharp again. "This room is designed to contain all noise. Feel free to explore."

With that, she turned and, seconds later, he heard the lock click.

This was a true measure of his desperation. He'd put himself completely at the mercy of one of his enemies. Who would be on the other side of that door when it swung open again? Mistress and the girl? Or O'Shea and the press?

He dropped his box on the floor—but the sound was muffled. Well. First things first. If he was going to be ruined, he wasn't going to be dressed like a workman.

The soap was of high quality, as was the cloth for his face. He washed and dressed in his proper clothes. He would be more comfortable with his hat but it hadn't fit in the box.

Once he had his tie straight and his moustache brushed, he began to explore the room. In addition to the sumptuous carpet—which went all the way to the walls—and the tapestries, the red settee was paired with a wing chair, the table between them holding an oil lamp that cast a warm glow around the room. And in the center of it all was an odd-looking leather ottoman. It was easily twice the size of a regular footstool and button-tufted. But that, in and of itself, wasn't particularly noteworthy.

However, there were metal rings affixed at regular intervals around the base of the ottoman and the leather was worn above those rings.

Gerard prowled around the edges of the room. Behind the tapestries along one wall—the wall with the door—blankets were hung, two and three thick. They must dampen the noise? He did a few experimental jumps, but the floor didn't even shake. How many rugs were beneath the top one?

For a moment, he hesitated. This room—while clean and well appointed—was wrong. Everything about this was wrong. He shouldn't be here, shouldn't be waiting on a madam and a whore. He needed to leave. This was a betrayal of everything he stood for. Everything he believed. Everything he *was*.

Then he saw the cabinet.

It was tucked along what he took for an outer wall. The cabinet itself wasn't fancy. It was a simple oak and wouldn't look out of place in a kitchen or even an office. There were drawers below the cabinet, like those that might contain the silver flatware.

What was a china cabinet doing in this room?

He tugged on the doors and they swung open on well-oiled hinges. But instead of china cups or stacks of papers, inside was a collection of...

Well. There was a riding crop and a wooden paddle. A long, thin cane was next to—was that a cat o'nine tails? A bullwhip was curled up next to a length of rope, next to a wooden spoon. At the end was a hairbrush, which seemed most out of place of all.

He stared down at the implements—he couldn't think of a better word for them—a strange mix of horror and fascination bubbling through him. No, it wasn't horror. It was...

"Oh, you found the cabinet already."

At the sound of a delicate, feminine voice, Gerard started. He spun around, slamming the cabinet doors shut and throwing his body in front of it.

It wasn't Mistress—nor was it O'Shea or anyone else who'd like to see him twist in the wind. Instead, it was... "Miss Bleu. You startled me."

It was only after he'd spoken that he realized she was holding a tray of tea things. "My apologies, sir." She set the tray down on the ottoman and stood, looking at him.

She was wearing a dress that bordered on demure.

Blue, yes—but a thin muslin today instead of a silk or a satin. The neckline was modest and the sleeves came down to her elbow. She had no jewelry on, no adornments at all. She looked prim and proper and at this exact moment, he was having trouble seeing how she fit into this place, much less with a monster like him.

He cleared his throat. "Is it nine already?"

"No," she answered quickly. "Almost eight thirty, maybe. I thought you might like some refreshment."

"That is very kind of you." Her cheeks dimpled at the compliment. When was the last time someone had looked pleased with him? It had been a long time. The women he surrounded himself with these days were just as severe and moralizing as he was. Compliments—and an appreciation of them—did not abound.

"Would you like me to serve you?"

"Where is your mistress?"

A divot appeared between Miss Bleu's brows. "She will join us shortly. I thought we might enjoy some time to get to know each other without her presence." But she still didn't sit, nor did she pour herself tea.

He took a hesitant step toward her. "Does she know you're up here?"

"Of course. There is little that happens in this house—or this town—that Mistress does not know about."

There was a challenge to those words that needled at him. "She has spoken at length about the need to keep you safe—yet she allows you alone with me?"

Miss Bleu considered this. "You may not believe

it, but I have a great deal of freedom. Mistress does not force me to do anything I do not wish to do."

He stared at her. "You're right. I don't believe that. Don't you want tea?"

"Yes."

He took another step toward her. "Then why don't you pour yourself some?"

The corner of her lips quirked, but any grin was fleeting. "I am waiting, sir."

"For what?"

"For permission, sir."

He frowned at her. "What do you mean, permission? Did you not just tell me you had a great deal of freedom?"

Miss Bleu gave him a long look then, her head tilting to one side as she studied him. He felt the hackles on the back of his neck stand up. "She was correct, then. You really haven't done anything like this before?"

He bristled. The implication in her words was not a pleasant one. "I will not let a mere whore question my morals. I have lived an honorable life." Without realizing it, he took another step toward her.

Her eyes widened as he advanced on her, but she didn't back up. In fact, she didn't actually look horrified. If anything, she looked... pleased?

"Why are you here?" he demanded, his words coming out low and threatening, even to his own ears.

"Because I choose to be, sir."

He was close to her now. Close enough to touch. "Don't mince words, girl. You know what I'm asking. Answer the question."

Something in her gaze flared and a look of defiance crossed her face. "And if I don't?"

36

He was breathing hard, he realized. Gulping in air like he was on the verge of drowning, hands curled into fists. He didn't have to look in the mirror above the washstand to know what he looked like. Mad. Possessed.

Dangerous.

And what did the slip of a girl do, when faced with his wrath?

She stood her ground. More than that, she lifted her chin in sheer defiance.

"You don't know what you're asking for," Gerard told her, his arms physically shaking from the effort it took to hold them in his side.

"Oh," she replied quite easily, as if he wasn't threatening her. "I know *exactly* what I'm asking for. Do you?"

"I see we're ready to get started." Gerard jumped at the sound of Mistress's voice as it floated into the room from the doorway. He hadn't heard the door open. Curse this soundproof room. "Sapphire," Mistress went on, "are you ready?"

There was a question Gerard wanted to ask, but he didn't get the chance. "I am," Miss Bleu, said, her gaze never leaving his.

"Judge Hobson, I'm going to model some behavior. Please, pay attention. I won't repeat this lesson. And above all, I want you to remember that we have rules and they will be enforced."

"Rules, I understand, madam. I am guided by the rule of law and also God's law."

Mistress sighed and even Miss Bleu looked bored with the statement. "Really, Gerard," Mistress said in a dismissive tone. "There is no need for such sanctimonious behavior here. Sapphire."

When she said the girl's name, her body tightened with tension. Or was it... Anticipation? "Yes?"

"Explain your limits before we begin."

"I do not allow knives. I do not play with blood."

Gerard recoiled in horror at the statement. "The very thought is repugnant. I could *kill* you."

Mistress looked pleased with this statement and the girl nodded her head in acknowledgment. "If you hit me in the face, please do so only with an open hand. I prefer to keep bruises off of my face and neck. I will not tolerate having bones broken."

His stomach turned. "What is it you think we're going to do here?" But even as he said it, his mind filled in an answer. He could see himself grabbing this girl—this child, really—by the jaw, slapping her to get her attention. It sickened him to admit that it excited him. This entire endeavor sickened him. He shouldn't be here, but it was too late. He'd surrendered and made the fool mistake to entrust himself to Mistress. He was at this very moment no doubt locked in this room with two women who had no concept of propriety, honor, or morality in any combination.

And for all of that, he wasn't sure he wanted to leave.

"Anything else?" When Mistress spoke this time, there was a crispness to her tone.

"If I say *no* or *stop*, you do not have to stop. If I cry, you can keep going. If I scream because you make me, you can be assured I am all right. But if I say *Billington*, you must stop immediately. There can be no exceptions to this rule. Therefore, you may not gag me until you and I are better acquainted."

Mistress nodded. "Ah, yes. I had almost

forgotten. We have not had to use that word in so long. Thank you for reminding me, Sapphire." She turned her attention back to him. "Those rules are, as she said, nonnegotiable, Judge Hobson. Do I make myself clear?"

Gerard stared at them. Were they both mad?

"Is there anything else I have forgotten, Sapphire?" Mistress asked, studying him closely.

Miss Bleu ducked her head immediately. "No."

The look in Mistress's eyes hardened and Gerard felt a skitter of something pass over his skin. Mistress cast him a knowing glance and said, "Pay attention." He didn't even have time to nod before she turned on the girl. "No *what*?" she demanded as she sank her fingers into the girl's hair and jerked her close. With her other hand, she gripped Miss Bleu's chin. Even at this distance, Gerard could see her nails digging into the girl's flesh.

It was terrifying to watch. Gerard was on the verge of intervening when Miss Bleu did something unexpected. She sighed and even at this distance, there was no mistaking that was a sound of happiness. Of satisfaction. "No, Mistress."

"You know how much I detest cold tea, girl." And then Mistress slapped her, right across the cheek. The girl's head snapped to the side, but Mistress held her still, her grip still buried into the blonde locks.

"What are you—" but that was as far as Gerard got.

"I'm sorry," Miss Bleu said, completely ignoring him. But then, how could she do anything but ignore him, when Mistress yanked on her hair, pulling her head all the way back and exposing the long line of her throat?

39

"I don't think you are, you little bitch. I think you've forgotten that you belong to me." She forced the girl to her knees and then slapped her face again. The girl's cheeks reddened, but her eyes hadn't even watered. Instead, she looked up at Mistress with something that was clearly devotion. Gerard didn't know what to do. All he could do was just stand there and watch this perverse display.

The girl's eyes rolled back into her head. "I haven't forgotten, Mistress." Her voice shook, but not with fear.

Mistress stepped to the side and threw the girl so that she sprawled on the floor. "I think you need to be reminded. It has been too long, Sapphire. Bring me... the crop."

Miss Bleu got to her hands and knees. "Yes, Mistress." And then, as Gerard watched in a mixture of sheer fascination and terror, the girl crawled—*crawled*, on her hands and knees. He stepped out of her way, but she pretended as if he weren't there. How was that even possible? He could do nothing but stare at her, the red mark on her cheek, and the way her hair now tilted to the side where Mistress had used it as a handle with which to drag her around.

This violence was unnecessary. It was wrong.

It was...

It was everything he'd tried to deny.

Miss Bleu stood and opened the cabinet that he'd been looking in. She removed the riding crop. Something that looked much like reverence made her gestures smooth and loving as she turned. She favored him with a wide smile, one that was reassuring and depraved all at the same time.

Was such a thing possible? Could she be happy that Mistress had slapped her and thrown her to the ground?

But he couldn't put the questions into words. Any hope of doing that died when she put the riding crop between her teeth like a bit and fell back to her knees. She crawled toward where Mistress was standing, hands on her hips, impatient in the middle of the room. When she reached Mistress's feet, she removed the crop from her mouth and knelt, the crop extended up to Mistress even as Miss Bleu's head touched the ground.

The girl was prostrate before the older woman, her bottom up in the air and the long line of her back completely undefended. A tumble of emotions flooded through Gerard and he had no hope of making sense of any them.

He had less hope of that when Mistress snatched the crop from the girl and brought it down upon Miss Bleu's bottom with an audible *crack*. "That," she said, bringing the crop down again with another *crack*, "shall teach you," *crack*, "to forget your place." Another *crack* and this time, the girl cried out in pain. Was her dress that thin?

Gerard took a step forward. But to do what? To throw himself over the girl in protection? To pull the crop out of Mistress's hand and throw it away? Or hold it in his hand, with the girl prostrate before him?

"Yes, Mistress."

He'd given up expecting this girl's reaction to match any normal response to a beating like this because she didn't even sound upset. The words came out as an exhalation.

41

Mistress ran the tip of the riding crop up Miss Bleu's back and then over her shoulder. Using just the tip of it, she lifted Miss Bleu's face until the girl was sitting on her heels, hands resting lightly against her thighs.

Waiting, he realized. For what? For another blow?

"I suppose that cold tea is better than no tea," Mistress said with a sigh as she lightly tapped the crop against Miss Bleu's reddened cheek. "You may pour."

The girl bowed her head and said, "Yes, Mistress. Thank you, Mistress." Then, still on her knees, she moved over to the tray of tea things.

"How do you take your tea, Judge Hobson?" Mistress asked as she settled onto one end of the settee, the riding crop balanced across her lap. When he was unable to answer, she looked up at him. "Judge? Perhaps you would like to join me? I can see that you have some questions."

He didn't miss the difference in the way that Mistress spoke to him compared to the way she'd spoken to the girl just seconds ago. The edge was gone from her voice. She was making an honest request of him. He did have questions. So, feeling both oddly numb and exhilarated, he stepped well clear of the ottoman and perched on the wing chair, as far from Mistress and the girl as he could. He didn't trust himself right now. It was no exaggeration to say he had no idea what he would do in the next minute. In the next thirty seconds, even.

"You may ask," Mistress said in that impossibly gentle voice of hers. "There is very little that you can do in this room that would be inappropriate or shocking, but I want you to feel that you can ask questions and know that they will be answered honestly."

42

"Why did you beat her?" It was the first question that came to mind, but it was just the tip of the iceberg.

Mistress and Miss Bleu exchanged a knowing look. "Because she wished me to."

Gerard shook his head, trying to make sense of this. "That's... that's wrong."

"And yet you did nothing to stop me," Mistress observed. "Nor did she."

Gerard looked at the girl. She held out a china teacup to him and he felt obligated to take it, even though he was not thirsty. Then, as he stared at her, she moved to Mistress's feet. Again, she sat on her heels, but this time, she put her head in Mistress's lap. Her cheek—the one that had not been struck—rested on the edge of the crop and almost absentmindedly, Mistress stroked her pale yellow hair. Without pulling her gaze away from him, the girl sighed and smiled, looking far too pleased.

"Thank you, Sapphire." Mistress continued to stroke her hair.

"I'm not sure he's ready," Sapphire said. "I think this is too much for him."

The statement pricked at his pride. "Ready for what? I would not brutalize a woman so."

The two women exchanged another one of those meaningful glances that was beginning to drive him mad. Carefully, Mistress said, "Isn't that why you came?"

Chapter Four

G erard couldn't look at them. He didn't want them to look at him, either, but there was no escape. So he stared into his teacup. "I'm not like that," he said, fighting to keep control on his emotions. Of anything.

Silence met the statement and eventually, he was forced to look up. The girl had tucked her hand under her cheek, looking so innocent. Except for the red mark on her face where Mistress had hit her.

He had the strangest urge to stroke his thumb over that red mark, see if it felt hotter than the rest of her skin. Would she flinch if he touched that spot? Or would she lean into his touch?

He was being ridiculous. Of course she wouldn't lean into his touch.

"Don't you ever get tired of that lie?" Surprisingly, it was not Mistress made this statement. It was Sapphire.

"I do not lie," he snapped. The teacup rattled in the saucer.

Sapphire pushed herself upright. For all the world, she looked like she was going to argue with that statement.

Mistress put a hand on her shoulder and spoke. "No one is questioning your honor. But we hoped to

44

show you that there are people in this world like Sapphire—people who need someone else to make the decisions, to take control of the situation." The girl nodded. Mistress went on, "People who need something more than gentle kisses and caressing touches. And does it not stand to reason that if there are people like Sapphire in the world, who give themselves wholly over to another person's needs, that there are then people who need the control? People who need to dominate? People who need to make the decisions and force people to submit to them?"

People like you. She didn't say it but she didn't have to. Everyone in the room knew that that was the unspoken sentence.

"I don't need to make people submit to me."

"Liar," Sapphire said in a soft whisper.

Gerard ground his teeth together, but he did his best to ignore her provocation.

She, however, would not be ignored. She pushed herself off of Mistress's lap and sat on her heels on the other side of the ottoman. "Who do you think you're fooling?" she demanded.

"I have no need to fool anyone." But even as he said it, he knew it was a lie.

"You've spent months—*years*—trying to make this town submit to your will and when you fail? Because you have failed, sir. You are lost." Her voice rose in pitch and she surged to her feet. "Lost in a hell of your own making, unable to accept what you are and what you could be if you weren't such a coward!"

It was the oddest thing. Maybe it was the room? She was screaming at him—he realized that on some level that felt detached from the man he'd been before he'd slunk into this room. The color seemed to bleed out of the room—his vision darkening on the edges until it narrowed on nothing but her.

Her mouth hung open—but he couldn't hear anything coming out of it. Her eyes widened in surprise, fear dancing at the edges and he realized that he was standing before her, his hand on her throat.

Squeezing. God, it felt so good. Warmth raced through his limbs and he wanted to give himself over to it.

"What did you say?" Even to his own ears, his voice sounded terrifying.

For so many years, he'd kept this locked away, this anger. This *need*. And she was right, damn her. He'd failed.

"Coward," she wheezed. Her hands came up and she clawed at his wrist—but she didn't pull him away.

He was powerless to let her go. "I could hurt you."

Something flashed in her eyes she smiled—*smiled*, dammit all. He simply did not understand why she wasn't scared.

Then he felt something in her body change—something tighten. As if she were strengthening herself from the inside out. Strong, he thought. God, she was so strong.

Her tongue traced her lower lip and then she pushed herself against his hand. "I don't think you can."

On some level, he was aware that she was goading him and he was aware that he was letting her. But the rational part of his brain was no longer in control.

Surrender. He surrendered to her.

So this was freedom.

"Are you going to let her talk to you like that?"

The clear, precise voice of Mistress floated through his mind.

"I could hurt her," he repeated, staring at where the darker skin of his fingertips dug into the milky white smoothness of her neck.

"She needs to be punished." The voice didn't come from inside his head, but he agreed with it. It was calm and logical. It was a good idea.

Slowly, he nodded and the girl's eyes got even wider. He flexed his fingers and lifted. She rose to her tiptoes and took in a labored breath.

"Hit her." It was half an order, half a plea.

"Hit me," she said in a strangled whisper. *Begged.*

He hesitated. It was his last grasp at sanity, or something that resembled it.

Sapphire's eyes narrowed. "You can't, can you? I knew you couldn't. I knew you were too weak for this. I knew—"

He threw her. Something in him—that last little bit of control—snapped and he threw her to the side. She sprawled out on the ottoman, the tea tray flying.

He bore down on her. "You should run."

"Do you want me to? Do you want to chase me?" When he didn't answer, she made a move to get up, but it was halfhearted at best.

He did what he'd seen Mistress do—he grabbed her by the hair and threw her down again. She sprawled out over the ottoman, facedown. He put his hand on the back of her neck and held her. "You should've run."

"What are you going to do to me?" she asked and, for the first time, he heard that note of fear in her voice.

47

If he were in his right mind, that note of fear might be enough to stop this madness. But it wasn't. He wasn't in control of his demons anymore. The inmates had run of the asylum and she was going to pay for it.

"Do you like her dress?" came the light comment. Mistress. He'd forgotten that she was in the room.

"It is too plain for her," he said, still holding her down. Her arms flailed and he captured one and stuck it under his knee.

"Then why don't you tear it off her body? She shouldn't wear things that you don't approve of."

Again, this seemed uncommonly reasonable. The dress was insubstantial. He grabbed at the neck and yanked. The fabric gave, exposing her back down to the waist.

"No, no," Sapphire moaned as the dress fell away from her shoulders in tatters.

Gerard hesitated, but Mistress's damnably calm voice was right there. "It's all right," she said reassuringly. "She can say no all she wants—but she can't stop you, can she?"

Gerard studied the skin he'd exposed. Her shoulder blades, her upper back were smooth, but upon closer inspection, he could see faint scars, white against white. The rest of her back was hidden by a rather prim white corset.

It was still more than he'd seen of a woman in so long. As if it were someone else, he watched his hand lift and stroke down the exposed skin. Lust. It wasn't strong—his cock barely stirred—but something that resembled desire stirred in his blood as he stroked her. Another feeling he'd kept locked away.

48

Sapphire shuddered under his touch and that was the most gratifying thing of all. He took what was left of the dress in both hands and tore it. She didn't have on a shift, but she had on a pair of bloomers that went almost to her knees.

She didn't get up, didn't try to squirm away from the violence. All she said was, "What are you going to do to me?" in that soft voice that shook.

"I…"

He didn't know. There had been something so satisfying about tearing her dress apart. There was still something so satisfying about seeing her lie prone before him, and knowing—or at least suspecting—that he could do whatever he wanted and no one would stop him. Not Sapphire, not Mistress and who else knew he was up here? No one.

"Sapphire." Mistress's voice cracked to the air like a bullwhip. "How do you address our guest?"

"*Sir*. What are you going to do to me, sir?"

Gerard looked over to where Mistress was on the settee. She sat primly, as if he hadn't torn a dress off one of her girls. She gave him a look that, louder than words, said, *well?* And then she extended the riding crop to him. When he didn't take it immediately, her gaze sharpened and she said, "It's all her fault, you know. Her and all of the girls downstairs—they're the reason you lost that election. And the election before it. No one in town wants to give up these whores. I own this town. I own these girls." She motioned with the crop to Sapphire. "I own her and it's all her fault that you are a failure of a man and a failure of a judge."

The words stung all the more because they were

49

true. Any normal whorehouse—he could've driven that out of town and made this place a moral, proper place to live. But Mistress's whores were too cultured, too refined—too *good*.

His hand closed on the handle of the crop. It was warm in his hands, the weight of it felt good against his palm.

"Sir," Sapphire begged. He didn't know what she was begging for.

This was it—the last moment that sanity had a prayer. Gerard felt like he was standing on a precipice looking down into an abyss that he'd spent his entire life trying not to slip into.

He could put this crop down, turn around, walk out of here and remain unchanged. The same as he ever was.

A failure. Frustrated. Alone.

A coward.

She squirmed on the ottoman, as if she were trying to raise herself but not succeeding. The next thing he knew, he'd brought the crop down over her backside. Even in this room, blankets covering the walls and carpets on the floor, the crack of leather against the flesh of her bottom, covered only with a thin cotton layer of her drawers, seemed to tear the air in two.

She gasped, a ragged sound. "*Sir.*"

He hit her again. It was easier this time. The motion was smoother. The crop whistled as it cleaved the air. There was no resistance until the whip hit her bottom. Again, she gasped—a noise that veered closer to a sob. The sound melted into him, a balm that soothed the irritation away.

This was him, sliding into the abyss of darkness. He closed his eyes and leapt. "Your Honor."

She stilled. "Sir?"

The crop cracked across her fanny again. "*Your.*" And again. "*Honor.*"

She cried out as he fell into a rhythm. It was savage, the beating he gave her. At one point, she screamed, "*No,*" and twisted off to the side, throwing one hand back behind her bottom to protect herself.

For the first time in what seemed like days, Mistress's cool voice broke through his reverie. "She has taken so much for you. Can you not give her a little reward?"

"Reward?" His voice felt rusty. He had no idea how much time had passed.

"Pain must always be followed by pleasure. She can only withstand the beating if she knows that, afterward, you will be there to comfort her and soothe her. If you pleasure her now, she will take more. She will take everything you have to give her, Gerard."

The words didn't seem to have the proper meaning and he didn't seem to have the capacity to put them in order. "I don't know... How?"

He was still staring at Sapphire. She was crying, he realized.

"You could start by complimenting her," Mistress said as if this were the most obvious statement in the world. "Compliments are always good, Gerard. You could pet her. Or you could go further. You could kiss her skin or touch her in intimate places. You could bring her to climax—the ultimate reward for her good behavior."

He stared down at the girl before him, his vision beginning to widen. He had a riding crop in his hand.

51

The girl—she was crying. She was in her underclothes and she was crying.

Because of him.

"Judge Hobson." The voice was less calm this time. "If you cannot do this, you will not be allowed back. Do not make me ask you again."

Gerard shook his head, as if waking from a long dream. He did not know if it was a nightmare or not. The girl was still rubbing her bottom, although her tears seemed to have trailed off. She still didn't run.

Why didn't she run?

Color reappeared as the darkness cleared and he saw it. Blood. A long, thin slash of red appeared on the white of her cotton drawers. He'd beaten her so badly that she'd bled. As he looked in horror, she turned her tear-streaked face to him. Except it wasn't her. It was Isabelle. It was thirty-seven years ago, the last time he'd let himself cross this line. God, he'd loved her. Loved her so much that it'd been inconceivable that she didn't feel the same. She'd said she loved him, too. Said she'd marry him. And he'd been so swept away with joy that he'd...

She'd run. Sobbing, Isabelle looked at him like the monster he was and, without a single look back, she'd run from him and right into Leopold Dupree's arms.

The riding crop dropped to the ground and Gerard backed up.

Sapphire—not Isabelle—pushed herself up and looked at him. "Your Honor?"

"I..." Tried to clear his throat. It didn't help. "I don't want to do this anymore. I shouldn't have done this."

Sapphire's eyes grew wet. "Did I do something wrong, Your Honor?"

He backed up some more, running into a wall. "You should've run. Why didn't you run?"

Wincing, she pushed herself off the ottoman and stood on uneven feet. Behind her, Mistress came to her feet, too. The older woman was scowling at him, but Sapphire was staring at him with concern. Concern! He'd done that to her and she was worried? About *him*?

"Why did you stop?" Her voice was so sweet, so soft. So damnably understanding. "I could've taken more, if it would have helped you."

He didn't understand. He didn't know what she was saying or why she was saying it and he didn't know why he'd whipped her. "Because I hurt you. Why are you here?" Why was *he* here?

"Because I choose to be here. I need the pain. And you..." She reached up and with the kind of tenderness she might reserve for a small bird with a broken wing, cupped his cheek in her palm. "I need you to give it to me. Don't fight this."

He didn't deserve her tenderness. He deserved to burn in hell. "But you're bleeding. You're bleeding because of me."

She smiled then, a watery smile that matched the tears in the corners of her eyes. "I can take it. I *want* to take it. Please, Your Honor."

He opened his mouth to say something, but there was a rock in his throat, a sharp jagged rock that made speaking impossible. His eyes began to burn. "You should leave me."

"Oh, Your Honor." She pulled him down and Gerard had no choice but to fall into her embrace. "You don't have to be alone anymore."

Chapter Five

Some moments passed before Mistress cleared her throat. "Judge Hobson," she said in a voice that was surprisingly gentle, Sadie thought. "You need to take care of her."

He nodded against Sadie's neck. Her skin was wet there. "I don't know what to do."

Sadie smiled to herself. That had never been more clear than now.

"Bring Sapphire back to the ottoman, please." Mistress had directed her comment to Judge Hobson, but Sadie did most of the leading.

Her bottom burned. She was going to have trouble sitting for a week, maybe more, but it had been worth it. Her body hummed with satisfaction—well, parts of it did. She wished that he hadn't stopped, though. She'd been so close to that space where pain lost meaning and she slipped into another skin. The rush of the crack, the smack on her flesh—it all fell away as pleasure and pain became one single entity that ruled her.

So close. So very close. Closer than she'd been in some time. His power—she shuddered again. Raw and untrained, but she couldn't help but to compare him to Jonathan.

She *needed* Hobson to understand the rules. Mistress had been right—he had the capacity to do real damage. Sadie was no green novice. She knew that he'd entered a separate place and had not been entirely aware of what he was doing. His demons had controlled him and she'd been at their mercy. They both had.

Once they made it to the ottoman, Mistress said, "Lay her on her stomach—yes, that's right." Sadie lay down, relieved that no one was making her sit at the moment. "Now pull down her drawers and see how you have marked her."

There was a long pause during which nothing happened. In all her years of surrendering to men and women, she'd never been with someone who didn't at least have an inkling of how to play. She'd been tied, burned, whipped, gagged, but never had the person with the whip ever broken down after beating her.

She wasn't sure she understood this man. He was so different. A man his age with these tastes should have had a pet for years. One that was bound to him. He could easily keep a woman happy if he admitted to his desires. But would he? Would he be able to accept what he'd done and what he no doubt wanted to do again? Or would he run?

Slowly, she felt the judge's hands start at the back of her knees, slide over her bloomers until they reached the top. Gingerly, she lifted her bottom into the air so that he could work them down her hips.

Then he gasped. "Sweet Jesus," he said in that stricken tone again.

"It's all right, Your Honor," she reassured him as the air hit the welts and apparently at least one cut. It had been a long time since she'd been so thoroughly whipped. She knew it was asking for too much, but the space between her legs throbbed with need that she knew this man would be unable to meet. Today, at least.

"I've seen worse," Mistress said dismissively. "You did a very nice job, Gerard. Look at how even those lines are." A soft finger stroked over a welt and Sadie winced, tensing involuntarily. "Such a good girl," Mistress said, running her hand over the whole of her bruised backside. "You did such a good job, my love."

Sadie exhaled. "Thank you, Mistress," she said, relaxing into the gentle touch.

"Judge Hobson, please go to the wash stand and get a fresh cloth. We can't leave her like this. We must tend to her."

There was another long, painful pause and Sadie knew that the judge was staring at her bottom with the same horror she'd seen his eyes earlier. She'd wanted to take the pain away for him, but she'd failed. "It's all right, Your Honor. I liked it. I could've taken more."

"Gerard." Mistress used the tone of voice that Sadie had no choice but to follow. "If you can't do this, you can't come back."

"Please, Your Honor," she encouraged, soft to Mistress's hardness. "I want you to come back."

"Why? I'm a monster." His voice broke on the word and she knew that he was crying.

She flung a hand out. "Please take care of me, Your Honor. I'm stronger than you think."

Fingertips lightly touched hers and then they were gone. She heard shuffling and rolled her head to see that he'd made it to the washstand. He grabbed a clean cloth and then came back and gingerly patted at her bruised flesh.

"Good," Mistress said in an encouraging tone. "Very good. Now come with me. In a drawer over here, we have a salve that will help with the swelling."

Sadie relaxed, folding her arms under her head. Her blood hummed through her body, making her pussy swell and throb. She wanted to touch herself, to take the edge off the need, but she needed permission to do that and she knew she didn't have it. If she tried, and if Mistress were still in charge, Sadie would be in so much trouble that she considered stroking herself just to see how far Mistress would take her.

But Mistress wasn't in charge, beyond what she was doing to educate the judge. He was horrified by what he'd done, but he'd done it, anyway. And Mistress had said that, as far as she knew, Judge Hobson didn't visit whores, didn't have a mistress on the side and had never been married.

If Sadie stroked herself off right now, he might break past the point of redemption. He'd either beat her to death for her sins or run and never look back. Neither outcome particularly appealed to her.

She settled for digging her fingernails into her skin. He still might not come back. He still might leave her like this because she'd failed to be what he needed.

"Smooth the salve on," Mistress said in an encouraging voice. "It's all right, Gerard."

Sadie turned her head to where he was standing. At this level, she could see that he hadn't even gotten hard. That was unusual. If not the sight of her exposed, then the violence itself should have aroused him. She liked a sound beating followed by rough sex. It was an ultimate release.

Maybe he couldn't?

He fell to his knees and, after another moment's hesitation, began to touch her. He smoothed the salve on with careful fingertips, wincing with her as she gasped at the worst of it.

"I'm sorry," he said in a numb voice when he glanced up and caught her watching him.

"You were magnificent," she assured him, but she wasn't sure it helped at all.

"Don't apologize for being true to yourself, Gerard," Mistress said with a sigh. "For heaven's sake. You should no more apologize to her for giving her what she so richly deserved than you would apologize to me for trying to put me out of business. The only difference is that I resist and she surrenders. And believe me, putting me out of business would do far greater harm to Sapphire than you ever could with a whip."

"I like your name," she told him. "It's pretty. *Gerard.*"

He dropped his head into his hands. "You are confusing me."

"No," Mistress replied crisply. "We are merely removing the veil from your eyes that you have insisted on hiding behind. The truth is before you. Look at *her.*"

To his credit, he did. This couldn't be easy on him. Sadie accepted that. Never had she seen a man struggle so much to find the path forward. Never had she seen someone so lost.

Not since she herself had been lost.

"I hurt you."

"Yes."

"You..." he swallowed. "You didn't run."

"No," she agreed.

"Why are you here?" For just a moment, she heard a little of his severity bleed back through.

"Because I choose to be. There's nothing confusing about it, Your Honor. I choose to be here. I choose to take the punishment. And I would willingly choose to do so again."

He eyed her warily. "Why?"

The salve began to work. Her flesh felt less swollen and the burning pain began to subside. So, too, did the frustrated climax that lingered between her legs. "Because I do not see your darkness as a curse, Your Honor. I see it as a great gift, one I would share with you."

"This is madness."

She couldn't help teasing him. He was far too serious. "Sanity is overrated."

At that, something unusual happened. The judge smiled. And in that moment, he became more than *Your Honor.*

In that quick, anxious smile, Sadie saw another man. She saw Gerard Hobson.

Her heart clenched as he held her gaze.

"Now," Mistress said, pulling them both out of their reverie. "Her dress is, sadly, ruined. Such a pity. I do have a nightgown here. Please pull her drawers back up and then help her dress."

This time, there was less hesitation on the judge's part. Perhaps that was because he was covering her

59

nakedness? Or maybe just because he was covering the welts. Whatever the reason, he pulled her to her feet and retied the string on her drawers before taking the white cotton nightgown from Mistress.

Sadie lifted her arms and let the man dress her. She always enjoyed this part, where she was coddled and cared for. Once the gown slid over her head, she smiled warmly at the judge. "Thank you, Your Honor."

"It seems we're in need of fresh tea," Mistress said, regarding the scattered remains of the tea service. "I'll just pop down to the kitchen and get more refreshments. Sapphire needs to drink and eat something after a session, Gerard."

He nodded once. Sadie turned to Mistress, who raised an eyebrow in question. Would she be all right, all alone with the judge?

She smiled. "Thank you for your kindness, Mistress." She didn't fear this man at all.

Mistress tilted her head in acknowledgement and then the door was locked behind them. "Would you care to sit, Your Honor?" She gathered up the remains of the tea set, wincing when her skin stretched as she bent over.

He sat on the far end of the couch and watched her. "I apologize again," he finally said, his deep voice sounding more sure by the second. "I gather that you have done this sort of thing before."

"Oh, yes." She finished stacking the cups and saucers and then stood a few feet away from him, waiting. Would he see that? Or would he miss the silent request for permission? "I have been here for years now and before that, I was on my own."

He looked at her for a long second. "Sit. Please," he added as an afterthought.

She beamed at him. "Yes, Your Honor. Thank you, Your Honor." As gracefully as she could, she folded herself at his feet, but she didn't touch him. She was, however, close enough to touch.

"I truly did not hurt you?"

She gazed up at him. Explaining this hadn't gotten any easier. If anything, she was worse at it now because she didn't have to explain. Mistress and the men who paid for time in this room all knew what they needed to know.

Sadie liked pain. She needed someone else to be in control. She'd always been wild—something her father had never understood. But she was the one who'd had to take control after her parents had died and she'd single-handedly found herself struggling to keep the Billington family from utter ruin.

"You *hurt* me, but you did not *harm* me. Does that make sense?" He shook his head. Of course he did. She shifted, her bottom stinging pleasantly so. "You could have done much more to me. You were in no danger of inflicting permanent danger."

"You don't know that."

"Actually," she said, "I do."

He leaned forward, his elbows on his knees and his head on his folded hands. He looked like a man in prayer. "I *do* not understand. I am trying so hard to understand how I can do such things and how you can let me but it makes no sense. It goes against everything I believe."

She considered this. "You don't have to understand it, you know. You just have to trust yourself and trust me."

61

"I put people in jail for what I did to you."

"No," she quickly corrected. "You put people in jail who do that to someone against their will. I was willing."

He looked up at her then. He was now at least as in control of himself as he'd been that night last week in his office. Perhaps he was even better, because he'd let go, if only for a little bit.

"Your Honor," she said, picking up his hand and holding it to her cheek—the one Mistress had slapped. "I *am* willing."

It was a long few seconds before his fingers curled into her skin. It wasn't a caress, but it was close. "Am I to believe she doesn't hold you here? That you do this of your own free will?"

She leaned into his touch. Strange, that now he should be so cautious when earlier he'd wielded the crop with brutal efficiency. Her bottom throbbed and that aching hunger began to build. "It's the truth, Your Honor. Mistress merely provides rules—rules I did not follow before she found me. If she hadn't brought me here and trained me properly, I'd be dead by now. Someone would have gone too far and I wouldn't have been able to stop them."

That wasn't the right thing to say. He pulled his hand back as if her skin had burned him. "I didn't kill that girl."

"I believe you."

His mouth twisted with displeasure. Was that because she hadn't added the *Your Honor*? Did he even realize he'd frowned?

"Why? You've seen what I am. You, more than anyone, should realize what I'm capable of."

62

She scooted forward and, without invitation, rested her head against his leg. He didn't push her away. "Because you stopped. When I said no. Which," she added, looking up at him, "you did not have to do."

"But you were crying." He hesitated, but then rested his hand on her hair.

She sighed at the touch. "That's why you didn't kill that girl. Because you stopped. And some men... they won't."

Silence fell over them as he processed that information.

After their last meeting, she'd gone back and read the newspaper article that implied that Judge Hobson had cut a whore to shreds. It had been like viewing a past she could have had—by all rights, the past she *should* have had. That was the fate that had been awaiting her before Mistress had pulled her off those docks and spirited her away to Brimstone.

The judge was afraid of what he could do and rightfully so. But reading that article again had terrified Sadie on a deeper level because she knew what *she* was capable of. She'd been chasing the pain, the surrender, but she hadn't understood the rules any better than the judge did.

She'd teased and taunted dangerous men who were far more willing and able to kill than Hobson would ever be, and when they'd hit her or held her down, she'd smiled at them, daring them to do more. Because she'd needed more. She knew now what she hadn't then. That she'd been courting death each and every time.

"I mussed up your hair," he finally said after some time had passed.

63

"It's all right, Your Honor." She looked up at him.

There it was—that smile again. It was small, as if he weren't sure he remembered how to express happiness with his lips, but devastating all the same. She wondered how many other people had ever seen that smile.

"There was…" he cleared his throat. "There was a hairbrush in the case. I could brush your hair for you." He blushed. Oh, heavens, Sadie thought. It made him look like a young man. "If you wanted me to. Mistress said I should comfort you…" his voice trailed off as she stared up.

"I'd like that. Would you like me to fetch it?"

"Yes."

Sadie got to her feet, wincing. Oh, she was going to be bruised. The reminders of this morning would linger for days and every time she sat, she'd think about being exposed to him. A shiver ran down her back.

She retrieved the hairbrush and carried it back to him. Because he hadn't asked her to, she didn't crawl. He did, however, raise an eyebrow when she sat on her heels, her back to him.

"I've never brushed a woman's hair before," he said.

"There are pins. Would you like me to remove them?"

"No." Then his hands were on her hair, burrowing to find the pins. "I… I should do this for you."

Sadie took a deep breath as his fingers worked through her locks, finding the pins and pulling them out one by one. He was methodical which was not a surprise, really. "That feels lovely."

"This is all right?" The brush began to stroke through her hair. He didn't pull or yank, either. Some men thought pain had to be laced into everything but that wasn't necessarily true.

"Of course."

"Mistress..." he paused, but Sadie waited. "She said that sometimes..." He cleared his throat and the brush paused. "As a reward... I should bring you to climax."

Every part of Sadie tightened down at the word, but she fought against the shiver. "Yes. That happens."

"Is that something you want?"

"Yes."

After another long moment, the brush began to move through her hair again. "But... how? How does that work?"

"It's difficult to explain—God knows I've tried. But the pain heightens my awareness, brings me focus. I can't climax without it. Regular sex is so..." she sighed. "So boring, really. And so few people know how to give me what I want."

"Really?" He didn't believe her. But that wasn't a big surprise.

"Yes. Like today, for example. You whipped me quite well. You could have pulled my drawers away and stroked my pussy with your fingers until I was calm again. Sometimes I climax from that alone. But the skilled masters—and Mistress is one—they can bring me close to climax and then leave me on that edge before they take the whip up again. Each time they punish me, they stroke me until I can't feel the

65

pain from the whipping anymore. I can only feel the climax struggling to be let loose and then, when they finally allow me to let go..." she shuddered, unable to stop the physical response.

For, truly, those were the best climaxes of her life. She lived for the ones where the pleasure and pain were one and the same, for the words, "let go, my pet," to set her free. Jonathan had been a master at it. He would thrust into her and refuse to let her go until he'd had his fill and then...

The brush moved slower now. Much slower. "That is..." he sounded horrified again.

She cut him off. "Please do not tell me it is wrong or immoral, Your Honor. I am what I am and God himself made me this way. As he made you, if you could only realize it."

She heard his throat click with a swallow, and then the brush began to move again. He tilted her head to the side to work a different section. Quite some time passed before he spoke again. "And this is what people pay you for?"

"Yes. Many are married men who would never raise a hand to their wives. They do not seek me out for sexual gratification. They seek me out to satisfy their darker urges." But just once, she wanted someone who wanted that sexual gratification.

Wasn't that what Mistress had asked her last week, after meeting the judge? What she wanted for the future? She didn't allow herself to think of marriage after Jonathan's rejection. The men she saw here were not for her. She couldn't give into her craven desires *and* be a wife. It was simple.

When he didn't say anything, she felt compelled

to keep talking. "Of course, they enjoy it." Unlike him. But she didn't say that part. "I am, after all, just a whore. Men pay to have sex with me. Some pay to tie me up and make me beg. None of it is moral. I understand if you can't do this again."

She couldn't keep the bitterness out of her voice when she said it. Because this was how it was, wasn't it? She was nothing more than a whore. A whore with tastes for pain, but still a whore. Men married good women and slunk into the Jeweled Ladies with their faces hidden. Good men didn't want to admit what they were. Not even to the women they loved.

He gathered her hair up and tilted her neck to the side. "I bruised you here," he said, his voice close to her ear. Then he stroked a finger over her neck. "I barely remember doing it."

She did. She'd done something she rarely did— pushed. And pushed. In fact, it hadn't been since before Mistress had found her that Sadie had pushed an unpredictable, angry man so far, just to see if he'd break. Which, of course, he had.

He'd grabbed her by the throat. Held her fast. For the first time in a long time, she'd been legitimately afraid. Not terrified, because Mistress was right there. But the fear at what he might do when he let go of his propriety had been real.

God, she'd missed it.

"I deserved it," she told him. "I called you a coward."

"You did, didn't you?" He sounded almost amused. "Very few would be brave enough to do that to my face."

"Certainly not. You are, after all, Judge Hobson."

The brush moved through her hair. "I tore your dress."

What was he doing? Cataloging his list of sins so he could repent tomorrow in church? Of course he was. Everything about this, including brushing her hair, no doubt, was a sin. "I have others."

"I'll buy you a new one."

That sounded like he wanted to see her again. Sadie fought to contain her excitement. But even that statement reminded her how very little he understood what was happening here. "I realize you might not know this, but my time in this room costs rather more than what the other girls might make for more regular visits. I can afford dresses." And, if Mistress was correct and he would easily pay double or even triple what she normally commanded, Sadie would be able to buy several dresses to replace that one. She'd never liked that dress anyway.

His hands fell away from her hair. "I don't know if I can do this."

"You already have," she told him gently, but she couldn't help it when her head dropped in resignation. He might want to see her again, but would he allow himself that want?

"I can't comfort you like that. *Sexually.* I—" He drew in a ragged sounding breath. "I have to draw a line."

Sadie rolled her eyes, knowing full well he couldn't see the movement. Whipping her was a fine thing to do because she deserved punishment, but Heaven forbid either of them enjoy it. Such was the morality of men.

What was she supposed to say here? That she

68

wanted it all? The pain *and* the satisfaction? Of course not. He would pay handsomely and she would just have to content herself with that. She ignored the hollow throbbing between her legs and instead focused on keeping her voice level. "You don't have to. This has been lovely. All of it."

A soft knock came and then the door opened. Mistress stood with a tea tray and suddenly Sadie was thirsty. "Ah, here we are." Mistress took in Sadie's posture and the brush in the judge's hands and smiled. "How nice, Gerard. Sapphire enjoys being pampered like that, don't you?"

"Yes, Mistress." She climbed to her feet and went to take the tea tray.

"You do realize, madam, that if you call me by that name outside of this room, I'll have you arrested?"

Sadie tensed, but Mistress just laughed as she settled into the settee. "You could try, I'm sure. But do not worry. What happens here will never leave this room."

She poured Mistress's tea and then offered some to the judge. "No, thank you. But please, have some. You should."

Sadie gratefully sipped the tea and moved to sit on the floor again. But Mistress said, "That will be all, my dear. The judge and I have some business to discuss. Della has some cookies for you in the kitchen."

They'd be discussing payment for services rendered, no doubt. Sadie straightened and looked at the judge. Then she waited.

One corner of his mouth twitched, but it was

69

nowhere near a smile. Then he stood and bowed to her. "It has been a pleasure, Miss Bleu. Thank you for your time."

That didn't sound encouraging. The more he came back to himself, the more she doubted he'd ever let himself get into that state ever again. Still, she could hope this hadn't been a one-time thing.

"I hope to meet again, Your Honor." She did her best to curtsy in the billowing nightgown and then took her leave.

Would she see him again?

Or would he be unable to get past his shame?

Chapter Six

Sadie heard nothing from the judge for a week. Then another week passed.

Mistress said nothing, either—other than to tell her that the judge had paid her eighty dollars and that Sadie's cut was fifty. She put almost the entire amount in her next letter to her sisters. The rest went toward a new dress.

She missed Abigail Whithall, the former Jewel who'd moved farther west and opened up her own dress shop in Virginia City, Nevada. Sadie's own skills with a needle were laughable and Mrs. Snyder, the wife of the dry-goods store owner, really only succeeded in making feed-sack clothes look slightly less like feed sacks.

Without Abigail, Mistress had resigned herself to doing what they'd done before—ordering dresses from New Orleans and tailoring them in Brimstone. Sadly, the mail between Brimstone and Virginia City was not reliable enough to order dresses from Abigail.

Two weeks after her morning with the judge, Sadie stood in the dry-goods store, trying to pick a dress style Mrs. Snyder wouldn't ruin beyond all recognition.

"A muslin, miss? You look lovely in muslin," Mrs. Snyder offered, pointing to a spring pattern that

71

was a confection of bows and frills. "With a sprigged blue print? It would complement your eyes," the heavyset woman said with a gleam in her eyes.

The Jewels did a great deal of business at the dry-goods store. They were some of the richest people in Brimstone and they spread their wealth around. Which mostly meant returning it back to the very people who had lined the Jewel's pockets in the first place. It was part of why the town refused to put them out of business. Mr. Snyder was a frequent guest of the Jeweled Ladies, although not one of Sadie's regulars. And Mrs. Snyder was either blind to her husband's faults or she loved money more than she loved fidelity.

Sadie eyed the dress plate cautiously. There were too many moving pieces there. Mrs. Snyder would never get the frills to lay flat if she had to bring the hem up. And she would. Sadie had always been a tad too short for the premade dresses.

"What else?" she said, waving the plate away.

Mrs. Snyder frowned at the dismissal and then straightened as if someone had poked her with a needle. Her eyes widened as she stared at someone behind Sadie and then she backed up. "I—a new book! Came in the post! In the back room!" And without another word, she scurried away.

A smile graced Sadie's lips because there was only one person in this town who could invoke that depth of fear in an otherwise law-abiding citizen.

Judge Gerard Hobson.

"A new dress, Miss Bleu?" he said in a cutting tone.

"Indeed. My last one was... damaged." Slowly— she wanted to savor this—she turned to face him.

"*Your Honor*," she added, dropping her gaze and almost, but not quite, curtseying before him.

The judge frowned at her. "Do not look so pleased to see me," he said in a menacing whisper.

She quickly glanced around the store. People tended to keep their distance from Judge Hobson—not that she could blame them. No one was within hearing distance of them, even though the store was quite busy on a Saturday morning.

However, they had attracted attention nonetheless. Sadie quickly arranged her face into one of dawning horror.

"Better."

What was this about? Why was he contacting her here, in the dry-goods store of all places? For a man who wanted everything to be kept as quiet as humanly possible, this was a damnably public way to go.

Sadie felt the blush rise up, which was not a bad thing. People would see that he'd embarrassed her. What kind of game was this? Even her other regular customers never acknowledged her existence outside of the Jeweled Ladies. Judge Hobson was not the only man ashamed of his darkness. But he was the only man who ever fought it for so long and so hard. So why was he even talking to her right now?

She needed to look terrified. Judge Hobson ruled by intimidation, so she'd better damned well be intimidated. If there was one thing that Sadie knew well, it was what being afraid looked like. She dropped her chin and took a step back, bumping up against the counter. She put a little shake into her hand as she lifted it to cover her chest. She glanced up at him through her lashes and saw a look of approval in his eyes. But that was the only place she saw it. His mouth was a thin line of displeasure.

She almost smiled. Of course he would be good at creating a public appearance. He'd been hiding who he was for so long, he probably didn't even realize he was doing it. "Would you consent to see me again?" he almost snarled at her.

For all of her pretending, something warmed inside of Sadie. Previously, he'd gone through Mistress to arrange their meeting, but now he was coming to her directly. He trusted her. Oh, he might not be able to admit it to himself, but this was an open display of trust.

She bowed her head, trying hard to look contrite. "I would be honored."

"You are too kind, Miss. I shall make arrangements."

She inclined her head, but at the same time, she attempted an awkward curtsy that slid her farther away from him. He would either understand that this was part of the act they were putting on for the spectators or it would make him mad, and well, she kind of liked him mad.

Just then, there was a rustle as a woman said, "Let me through!" Mrs. Emmeline Dupree pushed her way through the gawkers and hurried to Sadie's side. "Judge Hobson," she said severely, sliding her arm through Sadie's.

Sadie wanted to laugh at this development. She dared not, however. To laugh would be to be found out. So, instead, she clung to Emmy's arm.

There were a few whispers around the Jeweled Ladies about how perhaps there was something else going on in the Dupree Mansion, something less than *proper*, but Sadie had not given those rumors much credit. As Emerald Green, Mrs. Dupree had been the finest whore. Now, married for almost two years, she made a truly respectable mayor's wife. She also made a formidable ally.

"Mrs. Dupree," Hobson said and this time, the rage was unmistakable.

"Judge Hobson," she repeated again, each syllable a pointed barb she flung in his face. "I see you have made the acquaintance of Miss Bleu."

He cast a dismissive glance toward Sadie's direction. "She has a name, does she? I thought you were all interchangeable."

Sadie did not have to pretend this time. She sucked in air through her teeth and stiffened with a barely concealed rage. For a moment, she'd almost forgotten who he really was—the man hell-bent on driving all sin out of this town. Would he still seek to destroy her? To destroy them all?

He glanced at her, but she couldn't see anything in the look.

"Have you read the paper today, Judge Hobson?" Mrs. Dupree took as menacing step forward, all but dragging Sadie with her. "You should. Another dent in your armor, perhaps. You hold yourself so high above the rest of this town that I shall do nothing but laugh when you fall."

Sadie realized that Mrs. Dupree was also shaking but not with fear. Fury drove her and Sadie had to wonder what, exactly, had passed between the judge and the former whore. Mistress had been quite clear that the man had never paid for a woman before. But he wasn't above intimidating them.

75

"The paper?" Sadie asked.

A note of fear sounded in her ears. She tried to push it away. Mistress had said she believed him. Sadie believed him. She'd seen him in a blind rage, unaware of who he was and what he was doing but he'd still stopped when she'd said no. The man who killed that girl four years ago——-he wouldn't have stopped. Sadie knew he wouldn't have.

So what was in the paper?

Mrs. Dupree turned a victorious smile in Sadie's direction. "The madam of that brothel has come forward. She has a description of the man she thinks killed that girl. I wonder if the judge might not find it like looking in a mirror?"

Sadie clutched Mrs. Dupree's arm harder. There were three possibilities as far she could tell. One, the judge had killed this girl and had done an exceptional job of hiding it for a number of years. Two, another man who looked like him had done it. The judge was distinctive, with his silver hair and his severe sense of fashion, but not unusual. Or...

Or someone was trying very hard to make it look like the judge was guilty.

She did not know which it was.

The judge's lips grew even thinner and in that moment he looked more like the man she'd met in his office than he did Judge Hobson. He *had* seen the paper, she realized. And that was why he wanted to see her.

So be it.

"My dear Mrs. Dupree," he said in a voice as sharp as Sadie had ever heard. "I'm sure your source is merely misinformed. I don't know who is spreading

76

these malicious, libelous rumors about me, but I will get to the bottom of it."

"The truth shall out, sir." Emmy turned to face Sadie again. "Come along, dear. There is safety in numbers."

Sadie had little choice but to go along with her old friend. She could not even spare a glance back to the judge. Instead, she cowered her way out of the store, doing her best impersonation of the field mouse frightened by a hawk.

Emmy hauled Sadie away from the dry-goods store, all but towing her toward the Dupree mansion. "Are you all right, dear?" she asked in a voice that bordered on motherly as they walked up to the giant front doors.

"I am fine," she assured her. She'd missed Emmy. Of course, she'd seen Emmy several times since she'd moved out of the Jeweled Ladies and married the mayor. But it wasn't the same. As Mrs. Dupree, she was a respectable woman and could not be seen often in the company of mere whores, no matter how close as friends they might have been.

Emmy called for tea and guided Sadie toward the parlor. She'd never been inside the Dupree mansion, although she knew as well as anyone in this town that it was a fine house. "Pardon the mess," Emmy said as she pulled the sheet from a settee. "Raymond has given me permission to redo this room more to my tastes. It hadn't been updated since before his mother had passed. Now," she said, guiding Sadie to the settee, "would you like to tell me what that was all about?"

"I take it the judge was having a rather bad day

and was looking for someone to take his frustration out on." Which was one hundred percent true but also wasn't.

Unfortunately, Emmy saw the distinction. Of course she knew what Sadie was. Emmy had never been able to take any sort of punishment. The two of them had had long talks when Sadie had first arrived in Brimstone about why Sadie needed it and why Emmy couldn't stand it. She too had once been brutalized by a man who didn't stop. Emmy had been found by Mistress near death after such a beating—the kind Sadie used to chase after. Again she realized how easily she could have been that girl, dead and forgotten until someone needed her to make a point.

Emmy gave her a long look. "*No.*"

Sadie did her best to look innocent, but she was sure she missed her mark. "'No' what?"

Emmy blinked at her several times, her mouth hanging open in a most unladylike way. Sadie dimly thought that if Mistress saw her Emerald Green in this state, she would be reprimanded for her undignified behavior. "My God," she said in a stunned voice. "It makes perfect sense now."

Again, Sadie considered her options. She could lie and protest that she had no idea what Emmy was talking about. But Emmy knew her too well and there was no good way to explain the truth and even less of a good way to explaining why. So, Sadie said nothing.

"Are you not terrified of him?"

Sadie shook her head. "You know me. Truly, rare is the man who actually scares me."

"But he..." Emmy put her hand to her chest and again, Sadie had to wonder what had passed between her and the judge. "I cannot believe Mistress would allow this."

Again, Sadie did not deign to respond. "Is your husband behind the articles in the paper?"

Emmy's eyes shifted. "I do not think so." She did not sound convinced about this. "Raymond has proven again and again that the judge is no match for him. I do not think... No. I believe that he would have no further need to humiliate Hobson. Indeed, I would consider it a dangerous thing to provoke the man. Which is why I thought I was rescuing you from his clutches at the store."

Sadie smiled. "You were wonderful. I thank you so much for your care."

Emmy sighed and sat back in the chair, looking defeated. "I should have remembered that you never want defending."

"Do you know who is behind the articles?" She shouldn't ask. She should let this entire conversation drift away to other topics. She was curious how Emmy was adjusting to life as an honorable wife after her years in a brothel. Obviously, she and her husband doted on each other. There was a part of Sadie that was jealous of their easy affection even as she wondered what truly went on behind closed doors.

Emmy shook her head. "Why? Surely, you'd agree the man needs to be taken down a peg?"

"You have the right of it. I agree that it is a dangerous thing to provoke him. But I fear that there may be something else going on and that it could..." She grappled around in her mind for the right words. "I realize that he is no friend to the Jeweled Ladies. But he has a place within this town and should he be removed from that place..."

79

Emmy studied her. "The Devil you know?"

Sadie nodded. She wanted to tell her friend all about it, but there were rules and perhaps the most sacrosanct one was not to violate the sanctity of the attic room. She could neither confirm nor deny a single thing about the judge that would put him or his secret in danger.

At least Emmy understood that on a fundamental level. After all, she too had her secrets. "Do you think him capable of it? Murdering a whore?"

"I do not know what to think, except that we would all be safer if whoever destroyed that poor girl is caught."

Because if the judge had not killed that girl, then someone else had. Someone who was still out there, perhaps looking for the next woman who wouldn't be able to say *no*.

She shuddered at the thought.

"On that, we can agree," Emmy said, sounding thoughtful.

"I need to know who's behind these articles. If it's someone trying to get rid of the judge, I understand that. But what if it was something else? What if it's someone trying to deflect attention away from his own actions?"

Emmy considered this. "I can ask some questions. But you must promise me that you will stay safe, Sadie. I do not trust the judge and I do not think you should trust him, either. And, to be perfectly honest, I think Mistress a great fool to trust him at all."

Sadie reached over and patted her friend's hand. "I know you do not understand. But believe me when I say that I am in no danger."

Emmy notched an eyebrow at her. "From Judge Hobson?"

Sadie lifted a shoulder and dismissal. "All I ask is that you keep your suspicions—which I will not address—to yourself for the time being. I would hope that you would no more question any conversations I have or have not had with Judge Hobson than I would ask questions about you and your husband. Or any of the other rumors that might have been passed along."

To her credit, Emmy did not so much as even blush at this implication. Instead, she laughed. "Oh, Sadie. You are a firecracker. How much longer do you plan to stay at the Jeweled Ladies?"

"There is no other place for me." She'd been telling herself that for so long because it had been the truth. It had never been a lie or a cover. It still wasn't. But today, sitting in this fine house, talking to a fine lady that used to be a prostitute, the statement filled Sadie with emptiness. Emmy had gotten out. She was *more* now, more than Sadie could ever hope to be. Sadie was ashamed to realize that she was jealous of her friend.

"I have had a letter from Abigail," Emmy said, deftly changing the subject. "Written in her own hand, even. Would you like to read it?"

Sadie nodded eagerly, relieved to move on to happier topics.

But in the back of her mind, she couldn't stop asking herself the same question over and over again.

What was Judge Hobson truly capable of?

Chapter Seven

Of course he'd seen the newspaper. Titus made sure that Gerard had a newspaper on his desk first thing.

And what had he done? Had he done a single thing to defend the honor that was being slandered so viciously in the press? Had he made a single move toward uncovering the real culprit of this crime?

No. He'd gone looking for the girl.

He'd spent two weeks convincing himself that he'd been wrong and she'd been wrong and most of all, Mistress had been wrong. He'd had a moment of weakness. That was all. He appreciated that the girl had been willing. But he was not the kind of man who needed to make a regular habit of taking a whip to her backside. Or her front side. Or any of her sides. He wasn't *that* person. He'd never be *that* person.

For two weeks, he'd managed to convince himself of this lie. It had been easy. Once he'd slunk away from the Jeweled Ladies, the slouch hat pulled low over his brow, he'd slipped easily back into his everyday life. He'd felt lighter, freer, than he had in… Well, it didn't matter.

The girl had told him that surrender was salvation and he'd felt saved. He hadn't thought about Isabelle.

Hell, he hadn't even thought about Raymond Dupree. He'd thrown himself into his caseload with renewed vigor. He was an instrument of justice and he wielded that justice with righteousness and fury.

He'd not allowed himself to think of why. To do so would be to think about those few hours in the brothel, and he couldn't do that. He wasn't going to creep up to the edge of the abyss and stare into the darkness again.

Then the newspaper had landed on his desk.

The madam of the whorehouse where the dead girl had worked now claimed that she remembered the man who'd cut her girls to ribbons. She'd given a description to the newspaper and damned if she hadn't described Gerard to a *T*. Which was, of course, impossible. What was this world coming too, that the only people who believed his innocence were a madam and a whore?

And just like that, his sense of peace disappeared.

He'd gone out for a walk to clear his head. Truly. Someone was clearly out to get him and, at the moment, Raymond Dupree was in Austin at the Constitutional Convention for the greater state of Texas. Gerard was reasonably confident that Hank O'Shea was there as well, but just because they weren't in Brimstone didn't mean they didn't have a hand in this. Although Gerard was a man with more than one set of enemies, the mayor and his right-hand man were at the top of that rather long list.

Then he'd seen *her* in the dry-goods store. He knew next to nothing about women's fashion, but the shopkeeper's wife had had fabrics and books out and it'd taken very little for Gerard to realize what Sapphire Bleu was doing.

She was buying a new dress. Because of him.

And once he'd seen her through the window, he'd been helpless to prevent himself from walking into the store, helpless from coming up behind her. Helpless from remembering the last time he'd seen her, when he'd stripped that dress off her because he didn't like it and he *could*. In that moment, he'd known that he hadn't gone for a walk to clear his head. He'd gone looking for her. He didn't want to think about what he might have done if he hadn't found her at the store.

She would see him again. And, weak creature that he was, he was going to go.

It was so tempting to keep lying to himself. So very tempting to tell himself that he was not going to go back to that brothel and tiptoe up to that secret room for the sole purpose of beating a girl.

"Don't you ever get tired of the lie?" That was what she'd asked him last time as he'd clung to his illusions of being a decent, God-fearing man. Those illusions kept him miserable. And letting go of them, even for an hour, had lightened the load on his shoulders so much that he wasn't sure he could go back.

So he didn't pretend. He'd asked permission to see her again and she'd consented. As morally repugnant as he found it, he was going to lay her out and inflict bodily harm upon her. He was going to think about ways that he could reward her for her sacrifice that didn't involve touching her. Maybe he should bring a gift? Women liked gifts, or so he'd heard. He could brush her hair again—that hadn't been so bad. But even as he mulled over these options, his mind kept turning back to one phrase. *"They stroke my pussy."*

She'd said it so casually, and maybe for her it was a casual thing.

What would it be like, to touch her like that? To slide his hands up between her legs, to feel the warmth of her very sex? To let his fingers delve into her hidden places, to make her moan with satisfaction even as he held her down?

He would do so inadequately, of that there was no doubt. He had no experience. In all honesty, he'd lived most of his life as a monk. But there was something to the image that assembled itself in his mind, the image of her bare, reddened bottom sticking up in the air and him slipping his hands between her legs, of listening to her cries of pain become sobs of pleasure. Of sliding his own cock between those soft legs of hers, burying himself in her again and again, holding her by her hair as he used her. Because she consented to be used. Of knowing that he could give that to her and, according to her descriptions, he could also take it away. Because that's what she'd said, wasn't it? That the skilled could push her up to the edge of her crisis and leave her there?

Control. That was what Mistress had promised him. He could get control of his life again if he could work out his frustrations on someone.

On Sapphire Bleu.

He headed back to his office after meeting her. It should've bothered him, that the mayor's whore wife had interrupted his conversation with the girl, that she'd slung the same accusations at him. But he was whistling as he headed back to his office. *Whistling*, for God's sake.

He wasn't sure he wanted to use the riding crop again. She'd said that she did not like knives and blood and he'd made her bleed. But there had been other implements—the length of cane, for example. Was there a way to wield that light, flexible tool without breaking the skin?

Lost in these thoughts, he ran nearly headlong into none other than Hank O'Shea. Instantly, he was on alert. "Mr. O'Shea."

O'Shea's eyes flickered over him. "Your Honor," the man said, his face unreadable.

It bothered Gerard that he hadn't been able to sway O'Shea to come work for him because the man was too smart for his own good, and by all accounts, had very few morals. Why he'd chosen to utilize his skills on behalf of Raymond Dupree, Gerard could never figure out. But other than that, Gerard had a good measure of the man. He was ruthless, intelligent and loyal. In other words, outside of Mistress and her promise of secrecy, Hank O'Shea was the biggest threat to Gerard in this town.

He decided to handle the threat straight on. There was a time for the delicate dance of politeness and manners, but sometimes, directness was a weapon in its own right. "I see that you have been quite busy, Mr. O'Shea."

Although Gerard could almost look O'Shea in the eye, the man dwarfed him in other ways. "Oh?"

Gerard made a dismissive motion with his hand. If O'Shea was behind this it wouldn't do to let him know how much the rumors bothered him. "All those attempts to link me to a murdered woman in Beantown? Your fingerprints are all over that." He forced himself to smile, as if this were all one giant practical joke between the oldest of friends.

If he was hoping to get a rise out of O'Shea, he was going to have to keep on hoping. The man looked at him blankly. "The truth shall out," he intoned in a voice that was almost holy sounding.

The mayor's wife had said the same thing. And although Gerard knew he could not let this man get to him, he snapped to his own defense. "I didn't kill that girl."

The muscle in O'Shea's cheek twitched. It was probably a smile of satisfaction at having gotten under Gerard skin. "That's not what it sounded like to me."

Suddenly, Gerard was tired of playing this game. He'd lost. Raymond Dupree, like his father before him, had beaten Gerard in every single contest. "You may believe what you wish, sir, but I did not kill her. I was never in Beantown during this time when she'd supposedly died. I have never—" He'd never been to a brothel before. Except now, he had. He'd lost that little bit of moral high ground he'd claimed as his own. "—Paid a woman for sex," he finished, because that part, at least, was still true. And it would stay true. "Not that I expect you to believe me. You're probably enjoying this spectacle all too much, aren't you? Let me make it plain, O'Shea—your illustrious mayor has won. I have lost. It is not necessary to further humiliate me and to continue to do so is both immoral and illegal. I will not stand for it."

He expected O'Shea to mock this declaration, to point out that there was no way he could prove his innocence. But the Irish man didn't. Instead, he unexpectedly leaned forward, his gaze fastened at the pulse in Gerard's neck.

No, not the pulse. At his necktie.

87

"That's a nice pin in your tie. Solid silver?"

Gerard backed up a step. "Thank you. It was my grandfather's."

"That a fact?"

"I wear it to honor him," Gerard explained, taking another step backward. This whole conversation was off. "He founded this town, you know."

O'Shea straightened, his brow furrowed. "Well," he said suddenly. "I have business to attend to. As I am sure you must, too."

Gerard raised his eyebrows. What game was this man playing? "A delightful chat as always, Mr. O'Shea. Give my regards to our illustrious mayor when you next see him."

O'Shea inclined his head and moved on.

Gerard stood there for a moment, trying to make sense of the odd conversation. What was happening to this town? What was happening to *him*? Because he'd actually admitted—out loud and in public, to O'Shea, of all people—that he'd lost. He'd shown weakness. He'd asked for mercy. He'd also spoken to a prostitute in public and arranged to meet her again.

Judge Hobson did none of those things.

And if he wasn't the judge, who was he?

Chapter Eight

This time, when Sadie opened the door to the room, the judge was not furtively peering into the cabinet. Instead of jumping and looking like a boy with his hand caught in the cookie jar, he was sitting in the wingback chair, his legs stretched out and resting upon the ottoman. He was impeccably dressed, as always, but there was something that was different about him this time and it wasn't just the book he held in his hand.

There was a sense of order about him. She could tell by the way he raised his head and watched her silently as she closed the door with her foot and sat the tea tray on the ottoman that he wasn't going to fight against his true nature as much this time.

"Good morning, Your Honor."

Underneath his well-groomed mustache, his lips twitched. A shiver went down her back because right now, he was a man in control of himself, and he was looking at her with an almost feral hunger in his eyes. Had he changed his mind? Three weeks ago he'd said that he couldn't cross the line and do anything sexual with her. Which was a disappointment, to be sure. But it was clear that he'd become comfortable with the idea of hurting her, if not with the idea of satisfying her. Moving unhurriedly, he set his book to the side and stood, inclining his head in her direction. "Good morning, Miss Bleu."

Here, in the privacy of this room, she allowed herself to smile fully. "I brought you some tea. Would you like some?"

"That would be lovely. No sugar." He sat as she poured. "Will Mistress be joining us later?"

Sadie nodded, handing him a cup and saucer. "I wanted to talk to you before she came in." She stood, waiting.

He did not keep her waiting for long. "Please, fix yourself a cup as well and have a seat."

Sadie worked in silence, adding an extra lump of sugar to her tea before she sat on her heels near him.

His eyes warmed in appreciation. "What did you want to talk about?"

Sadie took a sip of her tea, letting it warm her. It was, after all, still quite early in the morning. "You said something the last time we visited here—"

He snorted. "Is that how you're describing it?"

She gave him a baleful look. "You kept telling me that I should run and I wasn't sure if that was something you actually wanted me to do or not. So I thought we might talk now, before Mistress came in, about what you do want me to do and what you don't want me to do. I told you my rules last time," she went on as his eyebrows knit together. "It is only fair that you have your own rules as well."

He was silent and Sadie got the distinct impression that the question had caused him pain. "You are quite perceptive," he said, dropping his gaze to his teacup. He looked ashamed, somehow. She didn't want him to look ashamed. She didn't want him to *be* ashamed, for that matter. But she knew that it was too much to hope that he would come to grips with his dark desires after just one visit with her.

"Some people enjoy the chase," she told him. "There's no need to fear your desires. This is a safe room where we can act them out without incurring any real harm. Do you understand?"

His gaze bore into hers. "What are you saying?"

She shrugged, tried to keep her tone light. "As we already have determined, I enjoy being hurt. And that can be dressed up in several different ways. You could chase me around this room, grab me, hold me down and act out a rape upon me, if you wanted. Anything you wanted, as long as you stopped the moment I said *Billington*. And I know you would."

She'd lost him, she could tell. He looked at her with a mix of curiosity and horror. "You would do that?"

"I enjoy the pain, but I also enjoy a little bit of fear. It's the unexpected in it."

His mouth dropped open and she could feel her cheeks heating. "But that is just one example," she hurried to add. "I would hope that you would feel comfortable telling me what you would like me to do. Besides calling you Your Honor," she finished with a smile. "That was a most... instructive moment last time."

"I do not think I want to chase you. The only other time I ever showed someone what I truly was, she ran and I did not chase her and it..." The memory obviously caused him pain. He pressed his hand to his chest.

She reached out and rested her hand on his knee.

91

"It was a long time ago," he finished in a rush.

She had no trouble grasping what he'd really said. He'd revealed his true self to a woman and she had fled in absolute horror and it had hurt him. Deeply. So deeply, in fact, that he'd spent God only knew how many years fighting against that one moment of his life. What a shame. What a *waste*.

"I won't do that. But I want to make you happy." He notched an eyebrow at her. "Well, happier, anyway. But you must trust me."

At least he mulled over her words instead of dismissing them out of hand. That, in and of itself, was progress. He leaned forward and cupped her cheek. "Why are you here?" he asked, as if this was one of the mysteries of the universe and he had no hope whatsoever solving it.

She held his hand to her face. "Because I choose to be," she reminded him. "Why are *you* here?"

He was silent for a long time, but then he finally whispered, "Because I choose to be."

She couldn't keep the grin off her face, not even if she tried. "Then let us choose what we shall do together while you're here, Your Honor."

He leaned back, breaking the contact between them. "I want to hit you. But I don't want to make you bleed again. You specifically said no blood and I found that unsettling when it happened. Even though it was accident." He let out a strangled chuckle. "I am reasonably confident that makes me something of a hypocrite. I can't believe that I just admitted that I want to hit you."

She tilted her head to one side. "When you thought of this, what did you want to hit me with?"

92

He covered his eyes with his hand. "The cane, perhaps?"

"Oh," she agreed, for the first time excitement tightening at the base of her spine. "That would be lovely. I'm sure Mistress will help you wield it appropriately."

No sooner had she spoken than the door opened and Mistress herself sallied in. "Ah, Good morning Gerard. And Sapphire, I see that you have made excellent progress in learning how to serve tea properly to our guests."

Sadie ducked her head. "Yes, Mistress. His Honor and I were just talking about what we might want to try today."

Mistress clapped her hands together and then settled into the far corner of the settee. "Wonderful news. What conclusions did you come to?"

Sadie turned her attention back to the judge. She did not want to speak out of turn and answer for him.

"The cane, madam. I would like to learn how to use it properly, without breaking the skin."

Sadie beamed at him. He'd said it out loud—without even having to hide his eyes from the truth.

"This is what you wish, Sapphire?"

"It is." She answered Mistress, but she did not turn her gaze away from the judge when she said it. His lips did not move when she said this, but his eyes crinkled with a measure of warmth nonetheless.

"Then let us begin. Gerard?"

It was such a change from the last time she'd seen him, when he'd been all but cowering in horror and fear and desire. This time, he wasn't as terrified of his actions. There was a certain measure of resignation to him, though, that Sadie did not find alluring in the least. But it was progress, nonetheless.

"Did you order a new dress?" He said in a voice that had more of a knife-edge to it suddenly.

"No." That was all she said.

"No, what?" His voice was even sharper and she knew that smiling was the wrong thing to do, but she couldn't help it anyway. He hadn't forgotten the lessons of the previous time. "Wipe that smile off your face." He reached out, hesitated and then slapped her across the cheek.

Her eyes watered and she bit her lip to keep from moaning. "No, Your Honor."

He eyed her dress. It was colder today, and as a result, her dress was worsted wool. It would not tear easily and he recognized it. "Take that off."

She stood and began undoing the row of buttons that ran down her chest. As she did so, she kept stealing glances at him. She did not know a man who did not enjoy watching a woman undress for him. But Judge Hobson was not like most men. Would he find this titillating? Or would it just enrage him with such a flagrant display of sin?

Because of the cold, today she had on a shift underneath. She slipped the dress down and kicked out of it.

"Take that shift off," he ordered her.

"But I like the shift," she said in a plaintive voice. When he surged to his feet, she exhaled in relief.

"I said," he growled, stepping into her and grabbing the shift by the neckline, "to take it *off*." He ripped it from her body, the sound of the tearing fabric filling the air around her. The skin at the back of her

94

neck stung briefly as the neckline cut into her before the whole thing fell to the ground. She stood before him in her corset, bloomers and stockings.

His gaze dipped lower, to where her nipples were straining against the top of the corset. He sucked in a breath through his nose, his chest swelling. When his eyes worked their way back up to her face, she saw that they had darkened with something that was unmistakably lust. He *was* capable of it. The thought thrilled her.

"The next time I tell you to order a dress, you better damn well do it," he ground out through his teeth, grabbing her by her hair and hauling her against his chest. Her nipples went tight at the contact and a tremor worked through her body.

She would not get her hopes up. The odds of him touching her intimately—no, she would *not* get her hopes up. "And what happens if I don't?"

His nostrils flared and his grip on her hair tightened. "Is that how you want to play this, you little whore?"

Her breath caught in her throat. "No, sir."

Next thing she knew, she was flying across the room. She hit one of the padded walls and slid to the floor. As she tried to re-orient herself, the judge loomed above her. "Get the cane," he said in a menacing growl. "I won't tolerate disobedience like this."

She didn't run nor did she crawl. He hadn't told her to, so she got to her feet and skirted around him to get to the cabinet.

As she retrieved the cane, Mistress began to talk. "There are two ways to approach this, Gerard. You can

95

attempt to hit the exact same spot on every stroke. It will leave most of her skin unmarred and it can be wonderfully painful. But there is a risk of the skin breaking with all of the repeated blows. So perhaps we should go with the second option today."

"And what is that?" At least he didn't sound horrified, Sadie thought as she opened the cabinet.

"Evenly spaced strokes. You did such a nice job of it with the whip—and you couldn't even see where you were hitting because she still had her bloomers on. You could leave her entire back striped. Hitting her around her shoulders will be most painful and hitting below her ribs could damage her internal organs, so you must strike more carefully in those areas than on her backside. She can take quite a lot of punishment there." Sadie shivered at the thought. "Although you would need to remove her corset in order to appreciate your handiwork," Mistress mused, as if this idea had just occurred to her and she wasn't sure whether it merited attention or not. "But I understand if you don't want to do anything like that. She is still, at this point, mostly decent."

Mistress wants him to fuck me, Sadie realized as she carried the cane back to Gerard. She notched an eyebrow and held the cane out to him. The challenge was unmistakable. She was complying with his request, but only the letter of the law—not the spirit. She was not being obedient and they all knew it.

"Your cane."

He snatched it out of her hand, grabbed her by the hair, and spun her. Before she quite knew what was happening, he'd her bent over his knee and had landed a solid blow on her backside. She squealed. The bite of

96

the cane—combined with the effortless way he'd bent her over?

Oh, he could be so very good. If only he could surrender completely.

Bottom stinging, she found herself back on her feet. "Do you want to try that again?" he growled, pacing back and forth before her.

She rubbed at her backside. Oh, he was quite strong. He did not have the control to hit in one spot over and over again. Just that one strike would leave a welt. If he hit that spot more than three times, she would break. She *wanted* to break. She wanted him to be the one to break her. The memory of Jonathan prowling around her floated in the back of her mind. He'd moved with feline grace, looking for weakness. But for the first time in a long time, Sadie was having a hard time remembering exactly what Jonathan looked like. He hadn't been as tall or as imposing as Judge Hobson was.

"Sir," she tried again. Obediently disobedient.

This time, she was braced for the blow when it came. It was a dance they did, when he grabbed her and spun her around, bending her over his knee with his leg propped up on the ottoman. The cane bit deep and she flailed at his leg before he sat her up on her feet again.

"You haven't learned your lesson yet."

For the first time, he sounded pleased by this. Warmth flooded Sadie. She was making him happy. She was being *useful* to him. It was such a good feeling.

"Take the corset off."

All of her corsets fastened in the front. It just made life so much easier. Sadie loosened the ties until

97

the panels gave way. Then she shoved the whole thing down over her hips and stood exposed to him. She had, in her time, been naked in front of many men. In theory, this was no different. But being here with the judge—it was almost as if everything were happening for the first time for her, too. Because when he looked at her breasts, she remembered that he'd said he hadn't attempted to act on his desires except for once, a long time ago. And if he didn't keep a woman... for the first time, she wondered was he still a *virgin*? Because the way he was ogling at her breasts—it was certainly an option. Or even if he wasn't, he hadn't been with a woman in her state of undress in a very, very long time.

"That is just another area where you could choose to strike her," Mistress said, intruding into the moment that Sadie would've rather kept private. "Her nipples are very sensitive, so do not strike them with the same force you would her backside. But you may pull on her nipples, slap them or bite them. We even have some clamps..."

His mouth wide open, the judge reached out a shaking hand toward her bare breasts, but then he jerked his hand back and shook his head. "That won't be necessary."

Sadie sighed, trying to keep the disappointment off her face. *Right.* Nipples were probably immoral. But that didn't stop him from staring.

And then he moved. He grabbed her by her hair and threw her across the ottoman. Some part of Sadie's brain noted that Mistress must have moved the tea set because Sadie did not send it flying like she had last time.

She sprawled out on the ottoman, her upper body exposed and vulnerable. It had been such a long time since she'd been this excited.

"Say it," he said as the cane whistled through the air again.

Sadie gasped as the pain cut through her back. "Your Honor."

"Again."

She cried out when the cane hit her again. "Your Honor." Her skin burned, but he hadn't hit her in the same spot. He slowly worked his way down the right side of her back. Each crack of the cane made her cry out. And every time she cried out, he told her to say his title again. She opened herself, trying to breathe through the pain. He did as Mistress had instructed him—the blows around her shoulder blades weren't as stinging as the ones on her bottom and the cane just barely kissed her skin below her ribs. But it was enough, especially when he worked his way back down to her bottom again and really laid into her. Her body began to sing as her blood pumped. That space between her legs began to throb the need of release. God, how she wanted to let go.

She couldn't. Not yet.

When he hit a particularly sensitive spot, she couldn't stand it anymore. She twisted away, trying to shield herself from the next blow. "Stop, stop," she wept.

And, for a blissful moment, the beating did stop. In a daze, she rolled to her side and looked up to where he stood over her, the cane still in his hand.

"Remember, Gerard, she can take more, but she must know that you will care for her." Mistress's voice floated out of the haze, caressing Sadie's mind and soothing the pain. "Can you not tell her how good she's being?"

The judge crouched down next to her, and, after a brief moment's hesitation, reached out and brushed a strand of hair away from her tear stained cheeks. "Are you done yet, beautiful girl?"

Sadie sighed. As compliments went, it wasn't terribly good. It barely qualified for the designation at all. But coming from him, she knew that he meant it. She wanted to be *his* beautiful girl.

She leaned into his touch as his thumb stroked a tear away. Already, the sting was fading and all she was left with was the thrum of her blood and the heat on her skin. Shamelessly, she twisted so that her breasts caught his attention. "I want to come," she whimpered. "Please, Your Honor, let me come."

His fingertips tightened against her skin and then he pulled away from her. "No." But his voice sounded shaky.

She writhed against the ottoman, her new welts hitting the leather and stinging all over again. She cupped her breasts and ran her thumbs over the nipples, feeling the little electric shocks from the touch echo down her body to her pussy. They were nice. They would get the job done eventually. But it would be so much better at his hands. If he would just take control of her and give her what she needed...

"Please, Your Honor," she begged, arching her back and thrusting her breasts higher into the air. She spread her legs and angled her hips toward him. "You can fuck me. I want you to."

"No," he said, sounding more severe this time

and even that sent another thrill through her and she moaned as she plucked at her nipples. "Stop that," he ordered her.

The next thing Sadie knew, he grabbed her by the hair and flipped her over again. This time, he kept his hand on her neck and kept her pressed against the ottoman so that she couldn't touch herself. And then the beating began again, this time on the other side.

She flailed against his weight, crying and screaming *no* when the cane bit deep. She had no control of the situation, none, whatsoever. He was in charge. For the first time, he was truly mastering her.

"Please, Your Honor," she screamed when she could get a breath into her lungs. But he didn't let go of her neck and he didn't stop.

After a certain point, Sadie moved past the pain. She began to float inside of her body on a cloud of pleasure. Every part of her body was sensitized and warm, even between her legs. He was merciless and she was free.

And then he stopped. Maybe Mistress said something. Sadie couldn't tell. She'd gone into a different place, one that she only glimpsed rarely. It had been years since she'd felt this power.

"I marked you," she heard the judge say from some faraway place.

The pressure on her neck was gone. She reached blindly for him and he was there. He lifted her off the ottoman and clutched her to his chest.

"What's wrong?" Was there a note of panic in his voice?

It was Mistress who answered. Sadie had almost forgotten that she was in the room. "Nothing, Gerard.

You merely took her to a place that very few women ever get to glimpse. It is a good thing. You must take care of her now and help bring her back to herself. Hold her and caress her. Here, wrap her in this blanket. Tell her how good she was. Can you do that?"

Sadie managed to lift her head up to look at the judge as he enfolded her in the soft blanket. Everything was hazy around the edges, as if she were looking through a thick fog. But his eyes, dark and black, stood out.

Please, she said. Or tried to say. She wasn't sure she actually made a noise. She wasn't sure she could right now.

He stroked his fingertips over her tear-stained cheeks. The touch was so gentle that she sucked in a gasp of air. Then his fingertips began to move. Down over her jawline, tracing the edges of her neck and then to her shoulders. "I have never known a woman like you," he said, and something in his tone made Sadie think of a man about to jump.

And then he did. Not physically because where would he go? But he brushed his fingertips down over the top of her breasts and then around her nipple. Sadie moaned, the noise pushing its way through the haze.

He pulled back. "I don't… I shouldn't…"

"*Please*," and this time she was sure that she'd spoken the words out loud. "Please, Your Honor."

Her pussy was throbbing and she shifted to try to take the pressure off it. She needed to come so badly, but what if he didn't let her? It would be the sweetest of all tortures.

When she shifted, though, she felt something else. Something new. He was hard in his pants. Well and truly *hard*. There was no mistaking the hot length of his cock, throbbing nearly in time with her own pulse. She ground her hips down, the welts on her lower back aching. *Everything* aching. "Let me take care of you," she whimpered again as she reached for the tie around his neck with heavy hands.

The next thing she knew, her hands were pinned by her side. "No," he said in a strangled voice. "I'm supposed to comfort you."

"Touch her," came the gentle reminder from Mistress.

And then the worst thing in the world happened. Gerard Hobson blushed. It shouldn't be possible that a man like him was innocent but he was, on at least one level. "I can't," he said again and at least this time, he sounded truly sad about it.

Sadie wasn't surprised. He had said as much after the last time. He could not—*would* not—satisfy her sexually. She was so close, all it would take was a touch from him. All it would take was his permission.

"Please, Your Honor. May I come? I'll do it myself. You won't have to touch me. But please, please—I *need* to come." She wiggled against him, trying to find a place where there was relief from the pressure on her tight bud and the welts on her back.

"All she needs is your permission," Mistress said, telling the judge what Sadie couldn't. "You control her climaxes, just like you control everything else in this room. Will you give her what she has earned? Or will you leave her to suffer?"

At the word *suffer*, Sadie moaned. The judge still had her wrists pinned to her sides and she was helpless in his arms.

103

Suddenly, she was off of his lap, alone on the ottoman. "You may…" He stood, and Sadie's eyes fell to the judge's trousers, on the thick ridge now clearly visible. He wanted her. He wanted to touch her. Maybe even to fuck her.

His arms shook as he held them down by his side, his hands curled into fists. But he wouldn't let himself. He was going to cling to the notion of morality come hell or high water, and the water was getting pretty high.

"You may touch yourself," he said as if each word were a separate shard of glass, cutting him from the inside out.

"Your Honor?" she asked, propping herself up on her elbows and staring at him.

He exhaled a shaky breath. "Touch yourself, beautiful girl." He swallowed and took another deep breath. "I… I will watch."

Without breaking his gaze, Sadie untied the drawstring of her bloomers. Slowly, wincing the whole time, she worked them down over her hips until they fell away. Then she lay back on the ottoman, feeling the cool leather against her back. Her legs fell open and she dipped her fingers in between them.

She moaned. She was wet and throbbing as she stroked her fingers over her slick bud. With her other hand, she cupped her breast and began to tweak her nipple, twisting and pulling. She let her head fall back as she gave herself over to the sensations, but she didn't dare drop her gaze from his.

The judge stood before the ottoman, almost between her legs, his chest heaving as he struggled to maintain his fragile control. Sadie could see it chipping away at the edges. Sweat beaded on his forehead and his color deepened to a dark red. He looked as if the effort of standing still were going to kill him. But he didn't break. Somehow, she knew he wouldn't.

"Give her permission, Gerard."

Sadie wished that Mistress wasn't here. This felt too intimate for a third person. She knew, of course—with this only being the judge's second visit—that Mistress would never leave them unobserved. But Sadie didn't want her here. She shamelessly pleasured herself for him and him alone, thrusting her hips up to meet her own strokes. Her crisis hovered just out of reach. She needed—she *needed*—

"Let go," the judge said gruffly.

And Sadie shattered. A cry tore itself from her lips as everything about her tensed and seized up. Wave after wave of pleasure broke over her until she was completely drained, lying limply across the ottoman and panting heavily.

"Oh, God," the judge groaned. He fell to his knees and roughly pulled Sadie up into sitting position. She lolled against him like a rag doll as he buried his head against her neck and clung to her with a desperation that took her breath away.

She threw her arms round his neck and held him until his breathing evened out. She didn't know if he'd come or not, but in the end, did it matter much? He'd kept control and made her lose hers. She'd never felt so at peace.

"Her wounds, Gerard," came the gentle reminder from Mistress.

The judge nodded against her and pushed himself away. "Lie on your stomach, girl."

She did as she was told and, within moments, he was smoothing the salve over her back. She felt as light as a feather blowing on the wind, happy and peaceful. This was the kind of thing that she wanted more of. How would it be if she could find this bliss in the safety of a home she could call her own? If she had a husband she could share her meals and her bed with? If they had a family...

She pushed those heavy thoughts away as she drifted. She would not ruin this moment with foolish and hopeless thoughts.

The judge sat her up again and helped her into a clean nightgown, then wrapped the blanket back around her shoulders. She tried to pull herself together enough to be able to stand and serve tea properly, but she was surprised when the judge poured her cup and handed her a cookie. "Eat this," he said in a gruff voice.

Gratefully, she took the cookie and drank the tea.

Again, she made the move to stand, but she didn't get very far.

"Come here, girl," he said, as he pulled her into his arms and settled her back on his lap. "Let me take care of you." Already, he was working his fingers into her mussed hair, pulling the pins. Sadie curled into him, still floating. He was warm against her. The blanket was around her shoulders and she was safe and so, so happy. He was perfect and all she wanted to do was spend the rest of the day curled up in his arms, loving on him. She could make him so happy, if he'd just let her...

"It seems that the tea has grown quite cold," Mistress said, startling her out of her reverie. "I shall get a fresh pot."

Chapter Nine

Even now, Gerard wasn't fully sure he trusted himself.

He'd never, in all of his life, seen anything as wantonly delicious as this girl lying naked before him, pleasuring herself. He didn't know what made it more erotic—the way she'd looked or the fact that he'd so soundly beaten her and she'd *still* found pleasure in it.

He'd managed to regain enough control over his cock that he was no longer in danger of humiliating himself. But that wasn't true, either. This girl had been laid out for him, waiting for him to say the word that would set her free. And as much as Gerard had wanted to abandon himself to her, he hadn't been able to because there had been someone else in the room.

Mistress.

He was losing all of the moral high ground he had so righteously claimed for years. This was his second visit to a brothel. He'd not yet paid for sex, but he was still paying for a whore. He'd always kept his darkness private and now he was openly displaying it before two people. And he'd sworn to both himself and the girl that he would not touch her sexually.

He had not allowed himself to want in so, *so* long that the need took him by surprise and nearly unmanned him and he knew, deep in his dark soul, that he would not be able to fight this temptation much longer.

So he kept negotiating with himself. He was, after all, a man who'd spent his entire life in the service of the law.

"I don't know," he said to the girl as he got the last pin out of her hair. They scattered around his feet.

"What don't you know?" she all but purred like a kitten.

"For starters, how you can sound so very happy after what we've just done."

She laughed, a light and happy sound, and threw her arms around his neck. "Your Honor, I realize that I'm not a paragon of feminine virtue but that was everything that I have ever wanted from a man. The only way it could have been better was if you had brought me to completion yourself."

He looked at her doubtfully because he was fairly certain that was the sort of thing whores said to their customers all the time. But she seemed to take no offense. Her hands stroked the back of his neck and he relaxed into her touch.

"I want you most fiercely. You *must* realize how special you are."

Now it was his turn to laugh. "I'm not special. I'm a monster. I would've thought after *that*, you would realize it." He leaned her back and ran his fingers through her hair. "I don't think that I can do what you ask. At least..." He took a deep breath and tilted her head up to his. "I do not think I can do that in front of Mistress."

She gasped as he stared into her beautiful blue

eyes. "Are you saying you might one day want to join me on the ottoman?"

He wanted to—oh, how he wanted to. But there was something about that image that bothered him. "If we were to do *that*," he said ridiculously embarrassed that he couldn't even bring himself to say the words, "would we not be able to avail ourselves of a bed? A bed in private?"

Happiness filled her eyes. "We might. But I fear that may still be some time off. There is much for you to learn and Mistress would want to make sure that neither of us are in danger."

Yes. Some primitive part of his brain crowed in victory and he couldn't have even said what it was. "You're right. There is much I don't know. Watching you was very… educational."

Which was a gross understatement. Had he ever seen a woman like that? He'd heard other men talk about women, understood the words they used, but to actually see her like that, her fingers stroking a part of her until she was gasping and moaning…

He shifted her on his lap. "Very educational, indeed."

She laughed and he felt himself chuckle with her.

"Would you like me to brush your hair again?"

She nodded and scooted off his lap to fetch the hairbrush. When she settled at his feet, he took a moment just to enjoy this. Never would he have imagined that he would find happiness in doing something so menial as brushing a woman's hair. But he did.

However, there was something missing. "Would you tell me your name?"

He felt the tension move down her shoulders. "Will you tell me about *her*?"

"Her who?" But even as he said it, he knew it was a weak dodge. The thought of Isabelle should have caused him pain. He'd been smarting from that wound for the last thirty some-odd years. Right now? He didn't want that weight bearing down on his shoulders. All he wanted to feel was the way the silk of the girl's hair flowed through his fingertips as he methodically moved the brush over the shining mass of gold. "There is not much to tell. I thought I was in love and I thought she loved me."

She considered this. "But she didn't?"

He shook his head—not that the girl could see him do it. "I asked for her hand in marriage and she agreed and I was so excited," he said, sobering at the pain the memory caused, "that I..."

"Sadie," she said in a whisper that was so quiet he had to lean forward to hear it. "My real name is Sadie. But I've gone by Sapphire for years."

"Sadie." He let his tongue move over the sound, testing it out. Yes, it was a much better fit for her than Sapphire. "It's a pretty name."

"Your turn. Is this the woman who told you that you were a monster?"

He was momentarily shocked. "You are a smart little thing, aren't you?"

She looked over her shoulder at him, a sly grin on her face. "Was there a question?"

"Yes, she was the one," he said. "When she agreed to my hand in marriage I... I lost control. I kissed her roughly. I handled her roughly. I..."

The girl—Sadie—she turned around and rested

her head against his thigh. "It's okay," she said, pulling the brush from his hand and wrapping her fingers around his.

"I tore her dress." He forced a laugh, although it didn't feel funny. "Although after what we've done here, that was nothing, was it?"

She shook her head. "I have many more dresses that you can tear, Your Honor. But you see the difference, don't you? You have my full permission to rip anything I'm wearing from my body. In fact, it excites me when you do that. It reminds me I am completely within your power. But you did not have that from her and, no doubt, you scared her quite badly."

Slowly, he nodded. "I see the difference now. I did not before."

The full force of Sadie's smile hit him somewhere in the middle of his chest. For all that he'd put her through, she was simply radiant.

"I'm sorry she ran from you. You must've loved her very much to show her what you really were."

"I did. And losing her…" Losing Isabelle had fueled the last thirty years of his life. He'd fought Leopold Dupree every step of the way and, when the man had the nerve to die in a carriage accident with his wife, Gerard had transferred that vendetta to Isabelle's son.

For the first time in his adult life, a creeping sense of shame stole into his mind as he considered what he'd made of his life.

"Well," Sadie went on, kissing the tips of his fingers, "I, for one, am glad that she did not marry you. For her sake *and* for yours."

Gerard stared down at her. "What?"

111

"You would have been miserable, both of you. Everyone else who comes to this room with me, they're all unhappy because they were unable to admit to the person whom they love and with whom they share their beds every night what they truly want. They spend their lives living a lie until they can't take it anymore. And then they slink in here, tails between their legs and all of them—every single one of them— convinces himself that this time will be the last time, that after this time they'll be better. This time, I will cure them."

She sounded heartbroken about that last part. And suddenly, Gerard needed to hold her. He needed the physical reassurance of her warm weight against his.

He lifted her up and tucked her into his arms. He was gratified her arms went around his neck as she held him tight. "I have been miserable no matter what," he admitted.

"Perhaps. At least now, you have a better understanding of what you are."

"And what is that?" Because he had thought of himself as a monster for so long that it was difficult to just suddenly… stop.

"You're a man," she said simply. "You have a slightly unusual set of needs, but that doesn't make you a demon. It just means that you have to look a little harder to find the woman who complements your taste. That's all."

They sat there for a while longer as he let all of this tumble around in his head. They were running short of time. At any moment, Mistress would come back to the room, making polite noises about tea. She'd ask Sadie to leave and then ask for her money.

He didn't want that reality right now. He just wanted to sit here and hold a pretty girl and enjoy the feeling that she did not find him to be an abomination. He was just a man. It should've been lowering.

It was anything but that.

But the clock was ticking and he knew it. "What do we do now?" he asked, his mouth moving against the soft skin of her neck. It was not a kiss.

"A standing appointment, I would hope. I haven't had any special requests like this for a while. I think…" She took a deep breath and sat up straight, pulling away from him. "Again, I trust that you did not kill that girl in Beantown. But since those accusations came to light, none of my other regular customers have been around. I think they're all scared that word might get out and they might face the same level of scrutiny you are facing. And since they are all known to patronize this establishment publicly, their reputations would be at far greater risk than yours."

He notched an eyebrow at her and gave her the kind of look that made petty criminals quake in their shoes. "And these other people would be?"

But she was not intimidated. Instead, she just laughed heartily. "I shall never tell. I protect their secrets and yours. I only bring it up to mention that I haven't seen anyone else in a while and I miss this. If you wanted to schedule a standing appointment, I'm sure every two weeks would be ideal. It would give me plenty of time to recover." Her lips quirked. "And replace my torn clothes, of course."

Every two weeks. It had been two weeks between his first visit and when he'd gone to look for her in the dry-goods store. Then he'd had to wait another week

113

for Saturday morning. "I believe that would suit me. Would that suit you?"

It was such an odd feeling, making someone happy. God knew he was out of practice and he'd never had a gift for it to begin with. The last time someone had looked this pleased with him had been...Well, when Isabelle had agreed to his hand in marriage. And that happiness had been fleeting, at best.

This happiness could be just as fleeting. But there was always a chance that maybe it wouldn't be. There was still so much danger loaded in the situation. He was still at the mercy of Sadie and of Mistress. Someone was out there printing slanderous rumors about him. And the whole town seemed on the brink of moral decay. Decay he was actively participating in, but still.

"I'd like to kiss you," Sadie said, brushing her lips over his cheek.

He would *not* panic. "Why?"

She giggled. "Because you made me feel very good today and kissing is nice."

"You..." He took a deep breath. This wasn't quite panic but it wasn't quite excitement, either. Why could he watch her do such sinful things to herself but the thought of surrendering himself to that same pleasure struck abject fear into his heart? "You made me feel good today, too." Even admitting that basic truth was difficult.

"Good," she whispered against his skin and then she took his face in her hands and began to move in closer. She was going to kiss him. It was going to be lovely. Not sinful. Not *wrong*. But at the very last

114

second, as her breath began to caress his lips, he panicked. He couldn't do it and that realization disappointed him greatly. Before she could protest, he leaned up and kissed her forehead. It was a poor substitute and they both knew it.

She sighed and leaned into his touch. "When you are ready, Your Honor, I will be here." Then she pressed her lips to his cheek again, saving him the pain of having to look her in the eyes and see her disappointment.

It was not, by any definition, a wanton or wicked caress. If he had to describe it, he would've said it was *sweet*. This was something new to him, as well. He had not made room in his life for sweetness and suddenly, he wondered why that was.

The doorknob rattled just as she pulled away and in came Mistress, bearing a fresh pot of tea. Gerard was deeply embarrassed to be found in this embrace by anyone. Which was patently ridiculous because Mistress had watched him do much, much worse. But still, it bothered him that this exploration was for three instead of two.

Soon, he told himself. He still had much to learn—including about how a woman found her pleasure. And there was no one else in this town who could teach him. Had Mistress said something about clamps? On *nipples*? He would have to think about that.

His cock stirred. Oh, yes. He would have to think about that because Sadie had quite nice nipples...

"That will be all, Sapphire," Mistress said, dismissing Sadie.

He stood and bowed and she curtsied in return.

115

Then she grabbed her dress and walked out of the room, her head held high.

"Well," Mistress said, pouring him a cup of tea that he didn't think he was going to drink. "Have you and she come to an agreement?"

"I want to see her every two weeks." He didn't want to share her with anyone else. But then, it didn't seem like he'd have to, not if the rest of her customers were too scared to visit.

Mistress gave him a stern look. "I will not see you harm her. You must consent to my continued supervision. There is much you have yet to learn."

Gerard inclined his head. Sadie had said as much herself and truly, Gerard had no desire to inflict permanent damage. "I agree. But perhaps we can work toward the time when I see her alone?"

Mistress looked pleased with this. "If she wants."

A month ago, he wouldn't have believed any of this possible. He never would've thought that he would come to this place in his life—but here he was, anyway. And, if Sadie were correct, he would've wound up here anyway. The only difference was that he was not breaking a marital vow to his wife. It was nice that there was some sin he was not yet committing.

He was, undoubtedly, going to burn in hell.

But, for the first time, he understood why people danced in the flames.

Chapter Ten

And so they began.

"The goal," Mistress said from her usual position on the couch, "is to tie her tight enough that the rope chafes and she cannot wiggle free, but not so tight that her hands and feet go numb. You don't like that, do you, Sapphire?"

"No, Mistress," Sadie said, looking up at him with those radiant blue eyes of hers.

Gerard never would've thought that there would be so much to binding a person, but they had been at it for almost two hours. His own hands were chafed from the rope and he did not enjoy it.

First, Mistress had had him tie Sadie's hands in front of her. Then behind her. There had been a complicated pattern of weaving the rope around her arms to hold them straight out behind her. He'd repeated the same pattern around her ankles. He'd tied her ankles to her wrists and, when he let her loose from that particular arrangement, he'd tied her to the rings that were affixed around the base of the ottoman.

Behind one set of tapestries, rings had been hammered into the wall. It was through those rings that he was now, for lack of a better word, stringing her up.

Gerard caught Sadie's eye. She smiled encouragingly, which might've been just politeness on her behalf. Because he understood that being able to properly tie her up would eventually enhance the experience.

But right now, it was a pain in his backside. Sadie was still in her shift and, aside from a few quick slaps with his hand, he'd not worked through any of his frustrations yet. "Like this?" He left some slack in the ring that held her left arm just above her head.

"No, no, Gerard, are you listening to *anything* I say?" At Mistress's dismissive tone, Gerard rolled his eyes and Sadie stifled a giggle. "You will do less damage to her if she is secure. Leaving her too much room to flail about could be more dangerous than just hitting her."

With a sigh, Gerard undid the rope and tried again. "How's that?" But he wasn't asking Mistress. He was asking Sadie.

She gave the binding an experimental tug. "Quite good."

"Quite good what?" Gerard intoned, grabbing her by the jaw and slamming her back against the wall.

Her eyelashes fluttered. "Quite good, Your Honor."

He repeated the binding on her other wrist and then turned toward where Mistress was watching the whole thing. "Are we done yet?"

Mistress arched an eyebrow at him. "Impatient, are we?"

It was the kind of look that only inflamed Gerard's blood. In the past, that knowing smugness would have driven him into fits of rage and done nothing but renew his resolve to rid this town of Mistress and her devious influence.

Instead, he turned back to where Sapphire was strung up. Through the thin material of her shift, he could see the tips of her nipples poking above her corset. If they were alone, he would rip the shift from her body and feast upon her. But he could *not*. He'd already put himself too much under Mistress's sway. He couldn't give her one more thing to hold over his head. He could not, under any circumstance, perform with her watching. Never mind how much he might want to perform. He wouldn't allow it.

He may pay for a whore's time, but he did not pay for sex.

He walked over to the cabinet and selected the riding crop. He knew that they didn't have much time left. The town would be waking up soon and the longer he stayed, the more difficult it would be to sneak back into his own home unseen. He wasn't in the mood to waste any more time listening to directions from Mistress.

No, he didn't pay whores for sex. But this? He bent the whip in his hand, testing its flexibility. Sadie, from where she was tied to the wall, made a little humming noise of anticipation.

This was a line he was going to cross. Repeatedly.

For the next twenty minutes, he whipped the girl mercilessly. He gave himself over to the whipping just as much as she gave herself over to him. It was too short, but when he stopped, he no longer wanted to bury Mistress so that had to count for *something*.

Once again, Mistress left them alone. Gerard untied Sadie and caught her as she sagged. He carried her to the ottoman and then rubbed the salve into the welts he'd left on her before he settled her between his knees so he could brush her hair.

"You are frustrated," Sadie said as he stroked the brush through her hair.

"Yes," he admitted. "I understand the need for such lessons, but…"

"Next time will be better," she reassured him, which made him smile all over again. She was a very reassuring woman. "Have you given any thought to what you would like to try next?"

He thought about that for a while. He finished brushing her hair and then reached into the pocket where he'd hidden his gift for her. "I want to give you what you want," he told her. Which was something he was still getting used to, feeling that another person's happiness rested with him.

"You could…" She misunderstood him. "But I understand that you can't. There are some lines that shouldn't be crossed."

He didn't miss the resignation in her voice. "Must you be so reasonable?" he demanded, but even as he did so, he worked the comb into her hair. It wasn't anything fancy, just carved horn, plain of any other decoration. The best he could come up with on short notice without drawing extra attention to himself. For he was reasonably sure that if he waltzed into the dry-goods store and demanded that they order him a ladies hair comb set with sapphires, that gossip would be anything but idle. "There."

Sadie looked up at him with surprise and more than a little bit of joy in her eyes. Her hand flew to her hair as she ran her fingers over the comb. "May I look?"

He settled back in the settee, letting the smile float across his face. Every time he smiled at her, it felt easier. "You may."

She got to her feet and, after a moment to steady herself, moved to the washstand. There, she took the comb out and reset it into her hair, much nicer than he'd put it in there. He would never succeed as a lady's maid.

She turned to him, a huge smile on her face. "It's beautiful, Your Honor."

He stood and moved to her, touching the comb and letting his fingers drift down the side of her face. Her eyelashes fluttered as she leaned into his touch, but it was the only touch he could give her.

"Sadie, do you think you might call me Gerard?" He wasn't sure what prompted him to make the offer. No one called him Gerard. He was Your Honor or Judge Hobson or just plain Hobson. He was *never* Gerard.

Except in this room. Mistress had taken to calling him by his given name and he had a dim memory of Sadie saying that she thought his name was pretty. And he found he wanted to hear her say it.

Her eyes widened at the request. "All the time or..."

He shook his head. "After we have... visited." The words stumbled awkwardly out of his mouth. He still wasn't sure how to describe what they did here without sounding like a monster to his own ears. Honestly, it was ridiculous—*after I strip you naked and beat you mercilessly, please call me by my given name.*

Utterly ridiculous.

121

Which left him with no words except *visit* or *time together*. Woefully inadequate, but the best he could do.

She dropped her gaze as her cheeks colored prettily. How was it possible that she could still look so innocent and fresh? It was almost hard to see her as the same woman that he'd literally tied to the wall earlier.

"Thank you for the comb, Gerard," she whispered and he had the urge to pull her into his arms and kiss her soundly. He fought against it and kept his hands to himself.

"I'm glad you like it. Is it all right, if I bring you gifts?" Because he honestly didn't know. He paid for her time, but the last time he'd given gifts to a woman, it'd been part of the courting process. And he was not courting Sadie. Certainly not.

"Of course." She turned back to the mirror. "I shall treasure this."

Before he quite knew what he was saying, his mouth opened and words tumbled out. "May ask you a question?"

She gave him a sly look in the mirror. "As long as we can sit."

He led her back to the settee and pulled her into his lap, careful not to jostle the comb out her hair. "Does your family know what you do?" Because it was a question that had bothered him. There had to be someone who was concerned about her, if not her reputation.

Her head rested against his shoulder and he found he liked it there a great deal. "Why do you ask?" she finally said after a very long pause.

"I want to know more about you." He knew a great deal about the people in this town. Titus, his assistant, was a good bloodhound, if nothing else. If Gerard set him on the trail, the man could follow it well enough. But for all that, he knew very little about the woman he was currently holding. And that did not sit well with him.

It was only then that he realized that she'd gone stiff in his arms, holding her body slightly away from his chest. "Why?" she asked again.

There was something in her hesitation that scratched the back of his mind. "I am putting a good deal of trust and faith in you," he said, the words coming out more severely than he wanted them to. "And I would like to be able to say that you have the same faith and trust in me."

The separation between her body and his grew greater. "I... I told you my name."

He leaned toward her. "Correction. You told me *half* of your name. Tell me the other half." It was not a request.

She slipped off of his lap before he realized what was happening and stood just outside of his reach. "Your Honor," she said, steel in her voice. "It is unnecessary."

He stood, but she took another step away from him. And he did not want to chase her down. "Why? Why won't you tell me?"

She shook her head. "Whatever you're thinking, *stop*."

"Oh, are you giving me orders now?" The irritation within him began to build. It was dangerous, that irritation. It made him dangerous. And she, of all people, should know that.

123

"You should be asking about the families of women who may consent to be your wife. By the time we have finished our lessons here, you will know how to conduct a proper relationship with a suitable woman who is both worthy of you and who understands your needs, just as you will understand hers. That is my gift to you. Do not ask me for more."

He wasn't sure what he'd expected her to say, but that was most certainly not it. He blinked at her, trying to make sense of everything. "By the time we have finished our lessons?"

She took in a ragged breath, a crack in the steel of her armor. "I understand," she went on gently. "I do. You've been alone for so long and finally, you've found someone who does not treat you as a monster— because you are not one," she added before he could open his mouth. "But don't confuse trust and faith and acceptance with affection. We both know where that'll lead." She didn't meet his gaze.

"Sadie," he said, taking another step toward her.

She deftly stayed just out of reach and before he could give voice to any of the confused thoughts in his head, the door opened up and Mistress reappeared with tea and cakes. She took in the charged tension of the room, how Sadie and Gerard were standing, and cleared her throat in as an authoritative a manner as any woman had ever cleared her throat before. "Is everything all right?"

Sadie turned to her and dipped her head. "Fine," and Gerard could tell from the tone of her voice that it was not. "Shall I leave you to it?"

She had not asked him for leave, but instead had turned to Mistress. It was a clear reminder of where he fell in the pecking order.

She was hiding something. After all these years sitting on his bench, he knew when people were lying and he usually knew why they were lying. They didn't want to get caught. It was really just that simple

"Of course, Sapphire," Mistress said, her voice tight. Without a look back, Sadie slipped out of the room. Mistress turned to face him, the tea service still in her hands. "Would you care to explain yourself?"

Gerard shook his head. He would not be scolded like a schoolboy. "Not to you."

Mistress frowned and damn it all if she didn't look... concerned. "Is everything all right, Gerard?"

"Stop calling me that." He took a deep breath, trying to get control of himself. Because he did not have it right now.

Mistress was still staring at him. It bothered him that she would be worried about him. She was supposed to hate him and he was supposed to hate her and instead, they were bound together by his secret.

"I am fine," he lied. "I just feel like—like we spent more time on ropes than I wanted to today." Which was, undoubtedly, part of the problem. He'd had a scant twenty minutes to work through two weeks' worth of frustration and longing and anticipation. After so long denying himself this one thing above all others, today wasn't enough.

"I understand," and damn if the woman didn't sound like that was a true thing. Again, his irritation flared. "I'm sorry that we had to spend that time on these lessons, but it will be worth it, I promise you."

He was pouting like a schoolboy who got his knuckles cracked with the ruler and he knew it. "I appreciate that. I do," he added when she gave him a

125

look that said he had not been as convincing as he'd hoped. And then, inexplicably, he continued to talk. To this woman! Because somehow, Mistress had become his confessor, the keeper of his sins and secrets. "She told me her name was Sadie, but she won't tell me anything else."

"Oh," she said, finally setting the tea tray down. "I'm surprised she told you that much, frankly. I do not allow the girls to use their proper names here. They are my Jewels. They have no past and we do not encourage their customers to think of the future. We exist only in this moment, Gerard. Or, in your case, we exist only in a moment that occurs every two weeks. Nothing more and nothing less."

"I don't have to like that."

Again, Mistress smiled that knowing smile that made Gerard want to hit something. "Of course you don't. But that is the way we play this game."

That is the way you *play this game.* But he didn't say it out loud. Instead, he said, "I understand."

It was only hours later, when he had slipped down the back alleys of Brimstone and into his own house and once again had completed the transformation from shuffling laborer into Judge Hobson that he considered the rules *he* was going to use in this game.

He couldn't take Sadie. He couldn't pay for sex. He could not stroke her breasts or the space between her legs because if he did, his control might slip and he might humiliate himself in front of Mistress. Therefore, Sadie couldn't touch him, either. Outside of her sitting on his lap or him brushing her hair and smoothing the salve on her back, they couldn't comfort each other physically.

But maybe when they were alone… even then, he couldn't see himself giving into sin within the walls of the Jeweled Ladies. Mistress would know.

So he made an ironclad promise to himself that would test his control. He would wait until he had Sadie in his house, safe in his bed, before he acted upon his desire for her. Then and only then, would he allow himself to give into temptation.

But until such time…

"Titus," he said, summoning the man into his office. "I need you to find something for me."

"For an arrest?" Titus said, perking up like a puppy expecting a treat.

Gerard shook his head. "No. I need information. About a girl."

Predictably, Titus looked disappointed by this announcement. "Who?"

"Sadie." He smiled, going with a hunch. Sometimes, a hunch was all it took. "Sadie Billington."

Titus scratched his head. "Never heard of her. Want me to start in Brimstone?"

"No." He considered Sadie's accent. "Start in Kentucky. Blonde hair, blue eyes."

Titus took note of the few other important details and then the lumbering giant was off. Gerard knew he wouldn't see the man for weeks, maybe months. Titus was thorough, but that came with a price. He wasn't smart enough to do anything quickly.

With that, Gerard turned his attention back to matters at hand. Next time, he was going to tie Sadie up. And then he was going to beat her until they were both completely satisfied. Maybe with the cat o'nine tails. He couldn't allow himself to touch her breasts, but Mistress had said those fine nipples could be tortured, hadn't she? And Sadie... she needed release. He could give that to her by telling her how to touch herself, couldn't he? He could control her climax. Mistress had said so.

Yes. *Yes.* He would exorcise his demons without crossing that final line.

Those were the rules.

Chapter Eleven

After the visit dedicated to rope, Mistress had Gerard take up the cat-o'-nine-tails. Sadie was practically quivering with anticipation.

"While you can certainly hit her hard enough to see each individual tail imprint, we should be aiming for an overall redness. Especially if you're going to be striking her in, say, the breasts. Why don't you try it?"

And he did. The first blow was far too hard for her poor nipples and she screamed. Gerard fell to his knees next to her and held her until the pain had blurred away. Then he said, "Do you wish to continue?"

Sadie heard Mistress snort at this preposterous question. A true master might not ask. He would just simply continue. But there was a tenderness to Gerard even as he beat her. It was a special thing, that softness in him. For she was certain that no one else got to see this side of him. Just her.

"Yes, Your Honor." She arched her back in his direction, trying to graze his hand with her reddened nipples. "May I have another?"

It took several attempts before he found his stroke, flailing the tails across her chest. The pain sensitized her nipples, making them pointed and hard, which, in turn, made each blow sting that much more.

129

And when she thought she couldn't take it anymore, he untied one of her hands and said, "Touch yourself there."

Sadie cupped her breasts in much the same way that she had the last time he'd given her permission to touch herself. But he stopped her. "No. Just... just pinch your nipples."

She squeezed it between her fingers, the sweet ache of it all making her sigh with pleasure.

"Yes," he said, his breath ragged. "Pull on—*yes*."

Last time, he'd just told her to touch herself. But there was something more intimate about him directing her movements. The hollow ache between her legs built to a maddening pressure as she tortured herself for him, watching the tension in his body coil like a cat, ready to pounce. God, how she wanted him to pounce on her. But of course he didn't.

"Like that. Slowly." He took a deep breath and untied her other hand. "Put your hand between your legs. But don't let go, my beauty. Hold."

She put her hands over her bloomers and stroked herself, all while still teasing her nipple. "Like this, Your Honor?"

"Yes," came the strangled reply. But he made no move toward her.

"I can..." she rolled, reaching for his trousers. Because he was obviously aroused.

"No." The answer was swift. Just as swift as him grabbing her and holding her down as he flailed the cat o'nine tails over her back until she was helpless and sobbing. Then, instead of fucking her, he tended to her skin and pulled her onto his lap.

Once Mistress had taken her leave, Sadie tried

130

again. She didn't ask. She just leaned into him and brushed her lips over his. But that was as far as she got before he tucked her head against his chest and said, "If you keep that up, I'll ruin that nightgown just like I ruined your shift."

"Why won't you let me touch you?" she asked, curling into a tight ball.

"Because."

"That is a poor answer," she scoffed, shifting on his lap. His arousal was there. It had been there the whole time. Why wouldn't he let her take care of him? "And here I thought you were this brilliant legal mind."

Something hard flashed in his eyes, but it was gone in a blink, replaced by an off-center smile that only made her want to kiss him even more. "You are asking for it, little girl."

She notched an eyebrow at him. "What do I need to do to get it?"

He gave her a little shove. "Go get the brush. I'll see to your hair."

Sadie sighed, but she did as she was told. "What will it take to let me kiss you?" She sat at his feet, relaxing into the movement as he brushed. "We don't have to do anything else. Just a kiss."

He snorted. "You cannot expect me to believe that. You, of all people."

"You are avoiding the question, Gerard." She couldn't see him, but she could feel him smile at the use of his name. "I know you want me."

He leaned down so that his mouth was against her ear. "Alone, my dear. I want you alone."

A shiver raced down her back as he returned to

brushing. "We are alone. Right now. Mistress would not know."

"Wouldn't she? Would you hide it from her if she asked you for the truth?"

She scowled. This was about her last name, she realized. Her name and her family. She hadn't told him anything about her, and when they had parted, she'd asked Mistress for permission to leave the room—not him. And he was right. She wasn't sure she could disobey a direct order from Mistress. It wasn't in her.

He chuckled. "That's what I thought. We still have a ways to go, you and I."

It wasn't a reprimand, but it felt that way, all the same. "I just want to make you happy, Gerard."

"You do." She was lifted up and nestled back in his lap and he sighed, a noise of pure contentment. "Trust me, pet, you do. But I am a difficult man, set in my ways." She noticed he didn't use the word *monster*, and that made her heart squeeze with happiness. "It is enough, for now, that we do this. Watching you take your pleasure at my direction... it is enough."

It wasn't, but discretion was the better part of valor. What she wanted was his hands on her, not just for the pain but also for the release. But at least he was letting her achieve crisis on her own. The application of his morals was... selective, to say the least. "You will not touch me? To bring me pleasure?"

"No, my dear. Only to hurt you."

"And I cannot touch you to bring you pleasure?"

His hand stroked carefully over her back, then lifted to stroke her hair. "This brings me pleasure."

Thus was the morality of men. Of *this* man. "It's

132

not the same," she pouted. He had to be a virgin. He *had* to be.

"It's enough." His voice was a whisper against her hair. "It has to be." And once again, her heart broke for him all over again. Because that woman he'd loved had hurt him so badly.

Tears pricked at her eyes as he lifted her chin so she had no choice but to look into his. There was sadness there, as if he knew exactly how hard this was for her, but his voice held no trace of that emotion. "Those are my rules. Do you consent?"

As if she could turn him away. Imperfect as this was—as he was—she would still take his imperfections over nothing at all.

She lowered her gaze and then felt a little thrill when his forehead touched hers. "I consent. It would be my pleasure to see you again, Your Honor."

And so they went on.

*

"If you don't mind me saying so," Mrs. Snyder said, looking up from her books with a greedy grin on her face, "you've certainly been ordering a lot of shifts recently, Miss Bleu."

Sadie fixed her sternest glare upon the nosy woman. "And, if you don't mind me saying so, I pay you a great deal of money for those shifts, Mrs. Snyder—*not* for your observations. Unless you'd prefer I take my business elsewhere?"

Which was something of an idle threat. Brimstone may be growing, but it was nowhere near large enough to support another dry-goods store. But there was always the mail. And Sadie wouldn't hesitate to order her clothes from a catalog. Then, at least, she could order a dozen shifts without fear of judgment.

Mrs. Snyder paled and looked contrite. "Begging your pardon, Miss. I meant no harm. Let me get that newest book for you." She scurried off.

"I do so enjoy watching you put her in her place." Sadie turned to find Emmeline Dupree watching her. "She has it coming and more, no doubt."

"No doubt." Sadie made a gracious bow and then studied her friend. Emmy looked... different. She smiled so widely that she practically glowed. "How are you, Mrs. Dupree?"

Emmy's eyes crinkled. "Well. Amazingly... well." Her hand fluttered around her waist before settling on the handle of her parasol. "And you?"

Sadie's eyes narrowed and she cocked an eyebrow at Emmy. Was she...?

Emmy blushed and gave a slight nod of her head.

"My darling Emmy!" Sadie rushed to grab her friend by the hands and all but spun her around. "How—when?"

"You know how," Emmy scoffed and they both giggled like schoolgirls. "We can't speak of it here. But I am dying to talk to someone about it. Can you come for tea after this?"

"Let me finish my order and my time is yours."

Mrs. Snyder came back and nodded her greetings to Emmy. "I'll be right with you, Mrs. Dupree."

"Oh, I came looking for Miss Bleu. But thank you anyway, Mrs. Snyder. All I need today is a peppermint stick." When Sadie gave her a questioning look,

Emmy leaned down to whisper, "Helps with the sickness, just a bit."

Mrs. Snyder pursed her lips in disappointment but otherwise kept her nosy thoughts to herself. Sadie ordered three more shifts, barely a month's supply at the rate Gerard was tearing them from her body. Then, arm in arm, the two women began to stroll back to the Dupree Mansion. The day was warm and the sun had broken through the weak winter clouds.

"You must tell me everything."

"Only if you tell me why you're ordering shifts by the gross," Emmy teased.

Sadie laughed and then mimed locking her lips and casting the key away. "You know I cannot."

Emmy's head leaned closer to hers. "Is it... is it him?"

When Sadie gave her a dull look, Emmy exhaled in frustration.

"Fine. Do not tell me. Just assure me you are whole and happy, my dear."

"I am whole and quite, quite happy." She was, in fact, still a little sore from the last flogging. Her nipples were still quite tender and every step sent a frisson of delicious pain over her skin. And with every step, she thought of Gerard holding her down. "Quite happy," she murmured again, mostly to herself.

Emmy laughed. "I would have thought, after all those stories in... the..." Her voice trailed off and she came to an abrupt stop in the middle of the walk.

Sadie came to a stumbling stop, barely managing to catch herself before stepping on the hem of her dress. "Emmy?"

The crowds were out today, taking advantage of

the weather. They surged around the two women. Emmy had gone stark white, as if she'd just seen a ghost. Her arm, linked through Sadie's, was shaking. "Emmy?" she asked again. "Is it the baby?" she whispered this last part.

"Do you—do you see him?" she said in a voice that cut Sadie deep, desperate, and pitiful.

"Who?" Sadie stepped in closer and made as if she were straightening the bow on Emmy's bonnet.

"Saints preserve us, he's real. He's here. He's here!" With wild eyes, Emmy gripped Sadie by the shoulders. "I need Hank. Raymond. Hank!"

"Easy." She spoke soothingly, taking Emmy's parasol and made a show of opening it. In doing so, she blocked Emmy's face from the other passersby. "Who?"

"Him. The…" she swallowed, her eyes hazy with fear. "The one who left me for dead." She clutched at Sadie's shoulders. "Don't see him. If he comes for you, you must not see him. Promise me!"

Her terror was contagious. Luckily, Sadie had a lifetime of controlling her fear. It was not difficult to keep an easy smile on her face and her breathing even. "Emmy," Sadie whispered, "you must not let him know you recognize him. You have changed. He's not here for you, I'm sure." Which was not strictly true. But it was what Emmy needed to hear. She took a ragged breath and her eyes focused on Sadie's face. "Good," Sadie said gently, sliding her arm around Emmy's waist. "Now I'm going to lift the parasol and you're going to look at me. But describe him so that I may warn Mistress."

Emmy nodded. Sadie stepped to her side and lifted the parasol. "Look at me," she reminded Emmy before nodding to the baker's daughter. "Mrs. Dupree has taken ill and I'm just seeing her home," she announced to the world at large because there were far too many people about for Emmy's odd behavior to go unremarked upon.

They began to move. "Missing... missing a tooth." Each word sounded like a blow landed on poor Emmy. "On his left side. He's grayer now. Gray hair."

"More or less gray than the judge's?"

"Almost the same."

"Taller or shorter than the judge?" Sadie let her gaze sweep the crowd.

"Shorter. Barrel chested. Not attractive."

"Try to smile," Sadie encouraged. "Where did you see him?"

"The hotel. Oh, God, is he staying?"

"No, no. I'm sure he's just passing through." Then she spotted the man.

He had on an ill-fitting waistcoat and topcoat that looked as if he'd stolen them from a fine gentleman's clothesline. His beaver top hat had a shine to it that came from much use and there was mud at the cuffs of his pants. The whole of him looked like someone pretending to be a man of quality and instead just making a mockery of it. And, as Emmy had said, he was not attractive. He stood outside the entrance to the Golden Star hotel, affecting the appearance of a dandy. But his eyes... they were hard and cruel as they scanned the crowds bustling up and down the street.

"I see him. No, no, eyes on me, Emmy," she said quickly when Emmy's gaze started to drift back to the hotel.

"My hair," she moaned as she started to sway. "He'll remember my hair."

137

"Nonsense. Many women have red hair and besides, your hat is adorably hiding most of it. It really is a lovely hat, Mrs. Dupree. Wherever did you get it? Did the milliner here make it? I have been meaning to order a new bonnet myself." She kept up this stream of inane feminine babble as they passed the Golden Star. "But then I thought to have a new dress made first to make sure the hat would suit. Do you not agree, Mrs. Dupree?"

To an outsider, she and Emmy would quite look like a couple of well-kept wives, gossiping about fashion. Not whores. Sadie hoped.

They made it past the hotel and then it was but a few short blocks to the Dupree mansion. Emmy strained against Sadie, but she held her friend back. "We can't run. It'll draw attention."

"I feel faint."

"Breathe. In through the nose, out through the mouth. You can do this, dear," she cooed, keeping a firm grip on Emmy's arm. "You're strong enough to walk back to the house. There we go. Look how far we've come already!" It was rather like teaching her little sisters to walk all over again.

"I need Hank and Raymond."

"Both?"

"Both."

That was all they said about it. After some of the longest moments in her life, Sadie guided Emmy up the front walk to her house. She paused at the door, casually looking back down the street, but she didn't see the little toad of a man anywhere. Hopefully, he hadn't noticed them.

"You," she said, shutting the door firmly behind

her. She didn't remember the maid's name but it didn't matter. "Where are Mayor Dupree and Mr. O'Shea?"

The maid looked at her askance as she hurried forward to take Emmy's arm. "Why, at the office, miss."

"Go fetch them right now. Both of them. Do not come back without them."

"Miss?"

"Go, for God's sake!" The maid scurried, nearly clocking into the cook. "Tea. Mrs. Dupree has had a shock and needs to rest."

The cook took one look and said, "Yes'm."

"Upstairs or down?" Sadie rather doubted she could get Emmy upstairs. The woman was starting to sag.

Worse, she'd started to cry. "I want Raymond," she keened.

"He's on his way, dear. Just a few more steps to the parlor. That's a good girl." Somehow, she managed to get Emmy to the settee. They collapsed in more or less a heap, Sadie's arms around Emmy's shoulders. She held her friend tight as she cried.

"It was all a long time ago," she whispered into Emmy's hair. "You're not the same girl and he can't hurt you now." There was a difference between fear and terror. She hadn't known that when she'd been a girl, but she knew it all too well now.

"Don't let him hurt you, either. Don't let him," Emmy kept repeating.

"I won't." The cook bustled in with something that smelled a bit stronger than tea. "Drink this, Emmy dearest. And the men will be here before you know it."

Emmy drank and the beverage seemed to help.

139

"You must think me a great coward," she muttered darkly, dropping her head in her hands. "You would not be afraid."

"I think no such thing. You know your limits. There is no shame in having a different limit than I do." She rubbed Emmy's back. "Does Raymond know about the baby yet?"

She nodded, seemingly relieved at the subject change. "I waited until the doctor confirmed it. We're all excited. Children, Sadie! I didn't have any brothers or sisters. I guess we'll all learn together."

Sadie notched an eyebrow at this particular declaration, but she said nothing that would embarrass poor Emmy. The woman had been through quite a shock and might not be aware of what she was saying.

Moments later, the front door burst open and the mayor and his assistant came running into the room, chests heaving.

"Emmy, darling," the mayor said, falling at her feet. "Are you all right?"

Emmy began to cry in earnest again and her husband scooped her up into his arms. "Miss Bleu," he said. "I must see to her."

"Of course." But she was speaking to the mayor's back and then he was gone, hurrying up the stairs and murmuring sweet words to Emmy.

An unusual spike of jealousy hit Sadie in her chest. What would it be like to have a husband like that, a man who would drop everything and rush to be by her side? But such things were not for her.

She turned and found herself in the rather unsettling gaze of Hank O'Shea, the mayor's man of business.

"She asked for both of you," Sadie said and immediately wished she could take it back.

This man was tall and broad and sinfully dark everywhere the mayor was light. He had an air of danger to him that could be quite intoxicating. But, alas, he didn't patronize the Jeweled Ladies.

Something glittered in his eyes and she stiffened. "Aye, I bet she did. But her husband will take care of her." But then he broke out an easy smile that was almost completely believable. "Can you tell me what happened?"

So she told him about the man, Emmy's shock and terror at seeing him. She described his appearance and the way he'd been watching the crowds.

"You didn't see him follow you?" Mr. O'Shea asked carefully.

"No. But I wanted to get her inside. Her condition—it's delicate."

"That it is." He exhaled heavily. "All right. Here's what we're going to do. I'm going to find him and follow him. You're going to go to Mistress and describe him. She's going to warn the other madams in town."

"Should we tell Sheriff Cutler and Judge Hobson?"

At the mention of Gerard's name, Mr. O'Shea's face went hard. "Why would we want to do that, Miss Bleu?" His voice was dangerously silky.

She took a step back. "He can be trusted."

"No," Mr. O'Shea quickly replied, "he can't. He's to stay as far away from Emmy and Raymond as possible."

She opened her mouth to argue, but he cut her off.

141

"Not negotiable. We've had our trouble with him before. I won't give him the chance to hurt Emmy again. Do I make myself clear, miss?"

This was rapidly turning into one of those rare moments when Sadie wished she were not compelled to bend to the will of those stronger and more capable than she was. Because the order in his voice was unmistakable and, although she knew she could disregard it, it would be difficult to do so.

"Emmy wouldn't want you to involve the judge," Mr. O'Shea said again, trying to sound placating. Sadie got the feeling that this man didn't know the meaning of the word *placate*.

"Fine," she agreed, because that much was true. She'd seen how Emmy and Gerard had spat verbal bullets at each other in the middle of the dry-good store before. "But if something... happens, he'll need to be informed."

Mr. O'Shea gave her a suspicious look. "You trust him? He's a monster."

She squared her shoulders and glared up at him and down her nose as best she could. "Sir," she said firmly. "He is nothing but a man." She didn't like the way this man was looking at her, as if she were tainted by her association with Gerard. But if there was one thing she knew how to do well, it was level the playing field. "Allow me to congratulate the mayor and his lovely wife for their impending blessing."

She wasn't sure what she expected O'Shea to do with this slightly *unusual* comment, but his face breaking into a wide grin, a real one, full of warmth and handsomeness, wasn't exactly it.

"I shall be sure to pass that along, Miss Bleu.

May I escort you back to the Jeweled Ladies? I fear the streets might not be safe for a pretty woman alone right now."

"On that, we can agree, Mr. O'Shea." He winged out his arm and she took it.

The whole walk back, she worried at her lip. This man, in whom Emmy obviously put a good deal of faith, had asked her not to tell Gerard something. Sadie could, she knew. She was not beholden to this man for anything, but Gerard... Mr. O'Shea might not trust him, but Sadie did. Unconditionally. And to hide something from him... it left her with a sour stomach.

They were almost back to the Jeweled Ladies when Mr. O'Shea spoke. "And what, exactly, is the judge to you, Miss Bleu?"

She titled her head to the side, as if she were seriously considering answering the question. "And what, exactly, is Mrs. Dupree to you, Mr. O'Shea?" she replied after several moments.

"I'm sure I have no idea what you're talking about."

"Indeed." They stopped at the doorway to the brothel. Mr. O'Shea turned to look down into her face. "If I were making anything other than idle chitchat with a man in the employ of my dear friend's husband, I would extend my congratulations to him, as well. But as this chitchat has been most idle, I can obviously do nothing of the sort."

One corner of Mr. O'Shea's mouth quirked up in a smile that was gone before her brain had finished registering how handsome it made his face. "I fear I have made a grave error in judgment, Miss Bleu."

"Oh?" She refused to take a half step closer to the

143

safety of the door. Emmy trusted this man so that had to count for something, didn't it?

"Aye. I fear I have underestimated you."

She laughed at that. "It is a common enough mistake."

"And here I thought I was anything but common." His eyes warmed. "You will be careful, won't you, Miss Bleu?"

She patted his arm. "I am always careful."

Mr. O'Shea bowed over her hand. "Give my best to your Mistress, Miss Bleu," and then he was gone, headed back to the Golden Star with murder on his face.

Sadie watched him walk away. Hopefully, that squat man had just been passing through. Hopefully it was all a misunderstanding. Hopefully, the squat man would never set foot inside the Jeweled Ladies.

But hope didn't pay the bills, so Sadie went inside to warn Mistress.

Chapter Twelve

Tap lightly," Mistress admonished. "That is the most sensitive area of her entire body. Always treat it with gentleness and respect."

Gerard paced around the ottoman, studying Sadie from all angles. Today, he'd bound her wrists to her ankles. She knelt on the ottoman, her legs spread wide. Not even stockings covered her body today. She'd never been so vulnerable to him. As he passed behind her, he reached out and stroked a faint white scar across her bottom with the tip of the riding crop. It was the only permanent mark he'd left on her.

She shivered at his touch as her head lolled backward. "What are you going to do to me, Your Honor?"

He stepped away. That question was a bit facetious. They all knew what he was going to do. The riding crop was in his hand and as he met her gaze, he smacked it across his palm. Another shiver raced over her nude body. But he didn't hit her—not yet. What he was about to do, well, it wasn't crossing the line. And really, he rationalized, it wasn't that different from stroking the cat of nine tails over her breasts. Tapping the flat of the riding crop against her sex—it shouldn't be that different.

But it was.

He sank his fingers into her hair and pulled so that she had to look up at his face. Then, slowly, he brought the tip of the riding crop to rest against her sex. He'd seen her touch herself there several times, and every single time it thrilled him.

"Oh," she breathed. "Oh, yes, Your Honor."

There was something different about her today. She was a little quieter. More reserved, maybe? He wanted to ask if everything was all right, but again, not with Mistress watching over them. And Sadie had otherwise given no indication that she wished to delay their regular appointment. She'd gasped in delight when he'd ripped her clothing away and held still for him to bind her. And now? Now she was looking at him with excitement and he decided he was reading too much into it for now, she was not particularly quiet at all.

"You're enjoying this too much." He pulled the crop away from her front and gave her a light smack on the tops of her thighs. She whimpered. "Let's see how much you enjoy this when I'm done with you."

Even after all this time together, he still couldn't get over how luminously happy she looked when he said things like that. She looked like he'd given her diamonds instead of threatening her well-being.

"Gently," Mistress reminded him.

Gerard moved the crop back so that the tip was resting against her sex. He could see her quivering with anticipation. It was not exciting. He was not excited by this because he wasn't touching her. It was just the whip. This was absolutely no different than flogging her backside. Just another part of her person to torment, that was all.

146

He only pulled the crop a few inches away from her before he brought it back against the fullness of her flesh. She jolted as if she had been struck by lightning before her eyes rolled into her head and she let out a moan. For the first time, Gerard wished he could... *No.* She had specifically said that he could not gag her. But there was something to the idea of tying a cloth around her mouth... *Yes.* He would have to think about that.

"Very well done," Mistress said approvingly. "Again?"

Gerard needed no encouragement. Again, he tapped the tip of the whip against her sex and again, Sadie moaned. When he did it the third time, he studied her face carefully. He could see the shock of the pain move through her and then he could see it somehow, somewhere along the way, be transformed into sheer pleasure.

He wasn't touching her. He was only holding her by her hair. He may have walked up to the line, but he hadn't crossed it yet. This was not sex. It was not what he was paying her for. This contact—it was merely another layer of control.

A layer he was enjoying.

He trailed the crop up over her stomach and circled her left nipple. He kept circling until it went tight before he lightly tapped it with the crop, too. She tried to shift, but he held her fast.

"How much of this can you take?" He wasn't sure if he was asking her the question or himself. God, her body... it responded to his every little touch, both soft and hard.

"Your Honor," she gasped before he smacked her nipple again. "I can take more. Please, give me more."

147

"Bossy," he said but he couldn't help smiling when he said it. "Maybe I should just… stop."

Her eyes went wide with something that looked like true pain. "I'll be good," she said. "I can do better, Your Honor."

"Then don't make a sound. Not one sound or I'll stop." Her mouth was open and he was tempted, oh, so tempted, to slant his mouth over hers and shut her up with a kiss.

But then Mistress had to ruin the moment. She was *always* ruining the moment. "Very good, Gerard."

How much longer before he would be able to see Sadie alone? Before he earned the right to request her presence at his own home? How much longer before they could meet on his schedule, instead of Mistress's?

How much longer until Titus found something that Gerard could use?

How much longer until Sadie was his?

He pushed that last thought away. If there was one thing Gerard was, it was patient. Waiting year after year for revenge that had yet to come to fruition had taught him nothing if not patience.

So he returned to the present and the vulnerable, beautiful girl spread wide before him. To her pain and her pleasure, both held in the palm of his hand.

He continued to stroke her… it was hard to think the word *pussy*. It was an improper word and Gerard did not like using it. But it was the word Sadie used, and as it was her body, he acquiesced to her language. So he stroked and tapped her pussy with the tip of his crop, watching as she struggled to keep her noises inside of her. This was a different kind of torture than just tying her to the ottoman and beating her mercilessly. This was slow and careful. This wasn't so much him venting his aggressions upon her willing body as it was him learning something new about how she worked. If there was one thing about his time with Sadie, it was that it was all *highly* educational.

She made a noise, something close to a high-pitched squeak. It slipped out of her lips and, as he was looking at her when she made it, he saw the fear in her eyes. The moment the sound reached his ears, he pulled the crop away from her delicate flesh.

"What was that?"

"Nothing."

Gerard pulled his hand away from her hair and moved to where Sadie couldn't see him.

"Nothing, Your Honor. I didn't mean to—I..."

He didn't know what to do. He'd issued her a challenge and she'd failed. Had she? Or had she made that noise on purpose, to see what he might do when she did fail? What was the correct course of action here?

He didn't want to, but he found himself looking to Mistress for guidance. When she did nothing but give him a placid smile, he wished that he could take the crop to *her*. All those times she'd verbally intruded upon his time with Sadie when he didn't want her and now that he needed a word of advice, she was going to be silent?

"Sir? Your Honor?" Sadie did her best to look over her shoulder.

He grabbed her by her hair and brought crop down over the top of her thighs. "I see how you are. Can't even follow basic instructions." He cracked the top of her thighs again and she squealed. It sent a thrill of excitement through him and he struggled to rein himself in. "You want to make noise? Then I'll give you something to make noise about."

He would not break. He was the one in control here, not her. He began to stroke and tap the crop against her pussy again, ever so gradually increasing the pressure on her sensitive skin. To her credit, she tried to be quiet, but that wasn't important. What *was* important was that he showed her he was in control of this—of it all.

That he was in control of her.

Every time she moaned, he would pull back and smacked the tip of her nipple with the whip before immediately returning to the bud of her sex. He focused on keeping his breathing even and his strokes steady. He was in control of this. He was in control of himself.

"Do you want to let go, pet?"

The look in her eyes nearly undid him. Because he controlled her. He controlled this—*this*, of all the mysteries of the universe.

"Come for me, beautiful," he murmured, lowering his face to hers. Then he tapped her sex again.

"Oh, God," she moaned in a high, keening voice and then her entire body shook with the force of her orgasm. The first one he had given her directly.

He felt the release travel throughout her body, shaking him to his core. She stretched to reach his lips, but he pulled away and let his gaze travel down the length of her body. He could see where the folds of her sex were reddened from his attentions and he almost stopped. But then, Mistress spoke. "If you truly wish to punish her, you will keep going. Pleasure can be just as torturous as pain, Gerard."

Sadie was still shaking from her crisis when he put the whip back to her sex. This time, as he tapped against her skin, she cried out, her body writhing as if he were putting all of his strength into the blow. The only respite he gave her was to smack at her nipples again, but that was not much respite at all.

Within minutes, she broke again—louder this time. This time, he did not need Mistress to tell him to keep going. He held Sadie up. She was trying so hard to get away from him and he was *not* going to allow that. Each tap-tap-tap against her made her cry louder and louder. She struggled against her bonds, but he'd tied them well.

When the third crisis took her, she screamed and he wanted to kiss her open mouth and swallow that noise, take it inside of him and make it his own. But he couldn't. All he could do was keep going.

He tapped her one more time and it happened.

"Billington." It was a strained whisper, nothing more than a breath that escaped into the room still ringing with her cries, but he heard it all the same.

Jesus. He'd hurt her. He must have—he'd gone too far. So much for his control. Horrified with himself, he pulled away, but Mistress said, "It's all right, Gerard. Make sure she wants to stop."

Gingerly, he crouched down at her eye level. She was slumped and listing dangerously to one side, like a ship that had taken on too much water. Regret coursed through him and he untied her with shaking hands. He should have stopped after the second release. He'd failed her, failed to protect her from his darkness.

"Gerard," Mistress said in that tone that brooked no refusal.

He couldn't even bring himself to touch Sadie.

151

What if he made it worse? "Do you want to stop, beautiful girl? Was it too much pain?"

She pitched forward, her body crashing into his. A strange relief broke in his chest as his arms came up around her. She wasn't so terrified that she pulled away. If anything, she leaned against him even more.

"No," she said in a weak voice, breathing hard against his neck. "It was too good. I couldn't take it."

Too good? Too... *good*? His chest swelled with pride, which was yet another sin to add to his ever-growing list. "Shall I take care of you now, my pet?"

She nodded once, which sent what remained of her coiffeur tumbling around her bare shoulders. He brushed a strand away from her cheek and tilted her head back so he could look her in the eyes. They were glazed with what he hoped was satisfaction. He'd never attempted to satisfy a woman—certainly not like that. "You were so very good, my dear."

She sighed in contentment and looped her arms around his neck.

"Instead of the salve, just press a cool cloth against her," Mistress said.

Gerard frowned. He hadn't realized when he'd started this that he would have to physically touch her *there*, but he should've. Any other time he marked her, he had to touch the damage to make it better. But he'd never touched her there. That wasn't just walking up to the line, that was *straddling* it.

She started to shiver. He took her blanket and threw it over her before making his decision. He wet a cloth and pried her legs open. For a moment, he stared at the pink flesh made red by his assault. This was no different than touching her backside. Not different at all.

152

But to touch her *there…*

This was the price he had to pay. He covered her sex with the cloth and then forcibly closed her legs over it. There. That would be enough to soothe her. She didn't want him to touch her there anyway, not so soon after the assault. Instead, he busied himself by rubbing salve on her nipples; quick, light touches that did not cause the pink flesh to stiffen.

Not much, anyway.

Then he pulled the nightgown over her head, feeling inexorably better now that her body was covered. Sounding pleased, Mistress excused herself as Gerard pulled Sadie onto his lap.

He was glad she'd gone. "Are you all right, darling? I hope I did not go too far…"

She nodded, but she still felt like a rag doll in his arms. "That was *wonderful*," she breathed against his neck.

"But you said the word."

"And you stopped." He could feel her lips curving against his neck, and today, he thought that if she tried to kiss him, he might not stop her. "I know my limits. There's only so much I can take."

He found himself holding her tighter than he normally did. Perhaps that was because he was not worried about any other marks he left on her body. Her back, for example, was unblemished so it was perfectly fine to rub it with his hand.

"Are you all right, Gerard?" She sounded more like herself even as she curled into his chest and held him closer.

He wasn't sure, but he didn't want to admit that. "Why do you ask?"

153

Her fingers tangled in the short hairs at the back of his neck. "Because you brought me to crisis yourself."

He'd straddled the line he'd vowed not to cross. "I have allowed you to reach your crisis previously." Her hand was slowly working up the back of his head and it felt... nice.

"But you did it *yourself*." She shuddered with what he hoped was satisfaction. "I worry about you, you know."

"Don't. I'm past worry." By now, he should be brushing her hair. But he found he could not move her from his lap.

His head was tilting down toward hers and he couldn't have said whether he was moving it or she was doing it for him. "All the same, I will continue to worry about you. I think of you often. Quite... often."

He couldn't kiss her. He simply could *not*. Wasn't it enough that he'd taken her pleasure in hand? Well, with the whip in his hand? He didn't have anything else to give her. Didn't she know that by now?

Her thumbs stroked over his cheek. "Gerard..." she murmured and it sounded different when she said it this time.

It sounded like forgiveness.

He almost gave into it, into *her*. He almost surrendered the last sliver of moral high ground he could claim. All because in her eyes, he was forgiven. She took his sin and she did so willingly. But her words came back, too. He could not—*could not*—confuse acceptance with affection. Nor could he confuse satisfaction with affection.

That's all this was. Satisfaction. It was clouding

her judgment and his. And he was better than this. He had to be.

So at the last possible moment, he kissed her forehead. It was the best he could do. And for the first time, the thought upset him. Deeply.

He hadn't heard back from Titus. He still didn't know where this girl came from or who her family was. She deserved better than this. She certainly deserved better than *him*. If, as she said, there were other women in the world like her, then there were other men in the world like him. She ought to have a husband. She didn't have to live her life as a whore.

Maybe he could help her. If only he knew who she was.

"I brought your present," he murmured against the smooth skin of her forehead.

She sighed and he couldn't help but think it was in disappointment. "How lovely. Thank you, Gerard."

She went to get the hairbrush and he pulled the midnight blue shawl out of the basket that held his work clothes. It made her eyes sparkle when he wrapped it around her shoulders.

"Shall we continue on?" she asked after several moments of silence while he brushed her hair.

That was what she said. What he heard, however, was different.

For what he heard was *shall I continue not to tell you who I am and shall you continue not to kiss me?*

"We shall."

For now.

But he would find out the truth. And then...

Then she would be his.

Chapter Thirteen

The pounding on her door came with her name shouted in terror. "*Sapphire?*"

Sadie threw herself out of bed. It was nine o'clock on Wednesday morning and she'd been reading. It took quite a while to get the latest Dickens novel and when the book arrived, she read it cover to cover, several times over. It was a luxury, to loll in bed with no other demands on her.

The frenzied knocking continued. Sadie threw on a wrapper and opened the door. "Yes?"

Mistress was standing before her in a remarkable state of near undress. Well, she was dressed, but without the care that normally went into her appearance. She looked like she too had been roused out of bed before time and had not had the chance to put herself together properly.

When Mistress saw her, she exhaled in relief. "Oh, thank God."

"Mistress? What's happened?"

Mistress latched on to her arm and said, "Come with me."

She hauled Sadie downstairs and through the hall to her office. When they were inside, Mistress shot the bolt and put a fluttering hand over her heart. "The paper," she said. "On my desk…"

A numbing chill raced down Sadie's back as she moved to the desk. She almost didn't need to see what the paper said.

Dead girl cut to ribbons in Fort Adams.

"I thought—I was afraid—well, we haven't seen you as much," Mistress began. "We haven't needed to. You haven't had any other requests and the judge pays you more than enough that you can be highly selective, and well, I suddenly realized I hadn't seen you in two days. And I was afraid…"

Sadie skimmed the article. The girl was blonde, slim. Her eye color was unknown because…

It was too gruesome. She couldn't keep reading.

She felt as if she were moving through molasses as she sat in Mistress's chair and stared up at the older woman. Today, she looked every single one of her many years—however many they were. "I was resting," she said almost mechanically. "His Honor—on Saturday—it takes time to recover." And she hadn't wanted to see anyone else. Hadn't wanted anyone else to mark her. That was between them. "And we have rules. I wouldn't leave. Not without telling you."

Swallowing, Mistress came forward. "You wouldn't go with him?" Sadie shook her head. "Even if he ordered you to?"

Sadie stared at her. "You're not suggesting—you don't think—"

Mistress didn't truly believe Gerard to be capable of this, did she? She couldn't. She'd been in the room with Gerard and Sadie for weeks now, watching and monitoring, teaching Gerard how to dominate properly. How to listen to Sadie, how to care for her afterwards.

157

The man was not capable of this crime. Sadie knew him too well. He was *not* a monster.

The silence hung in between them. "I will make some inquiries. I will send a letter to the madams in Fort Adams. I *will* find out who did this." For a second, Mistress looked less like a terrified middle-aged woman and more like an avenging angel of justice.

"It can't have been him," she tried to reason. "I trust him. He wouldn't have done this."

Mistress frowned, her worry contagious. At least, Sadie didn't *believe* Gerard would do this. They'd spent almost three months together now. In that room in the attic, they had both been stripped away of any artifice. She knew what he was and he knew what she was and she trusted him and he put his faith in her. Not only did she not believe that he was capable of murdering a whore by cutting her to pieces, she…

She didn't want to believe that he would seek out anyone else. She desperately wanted to believe that he only came to her.

"Be that as it may," Mistress went on, sounding more like her regular self, "I do not want you to leave this house unaccompanied. Should Judge Hobson approach you on the street, I forbid you from going anywhere alone with him."

Sadie gave her a dull look. "I'm not a child. I understand the rules and why I follow them. And I choose to continue to follow them."

For a moment, Mistress softened. But it didn't last. "See that you do. Even if this is not Judge Hobson, this is a threat to us all. Fort Adams is only ten miles away."

Closer than Beantown. "What of the man Mrs. Dupree believes hurt her?" Because if they were going to look for a monster, that man would be first on Sadie's list of suspects. She shivered just thinking of how scared Emmy had been after catching a glimpse of the man.

Mistress nodded, looking visibly relieved. "Quite right. He moved on but he might have gone to Fort Adams. I *shall* find out."

But just then, the floor underneath them started to shake with vigorous pounding. "Open up!" came a deep voice. "This is Sheriff Cutler." This statement was followed by more pounding.

"Oh for heaven's sake," Mistress muttered, her hands flying to her hair. "Get dressed, dear. Tell the other girls to prepare for anything."

Sadie hurried. First the newspaper, now the sheriff banging on their doors? "Get up," she hissed as heads popped out of doors, worry on everyone's face. "We must be ready."

For the first time in a while, Sadie was truly afraid. And it was not pleasurable.

Fifteen minutes later, Sadie slipped into the already crowded parlor. Almost everyone was there and, considering how very little time they'd had to get dressed, everyone looked more or less presentable. Even Mistress had somehow managed to go from looking like a frazzled woman of her years to looking remarkably like Mistress.

Her Jewels were lined up on one side of the parlor, looking very much like a rainbow on display after a storm cloud had finished its downpour. A few of the girls looked nervous but several had turned on the charm. The only person missing was Sterling Silver, because the bartender did not live at the brothel. Otherwise, they were all here.

Any and all sensuality was aimed squarely at the other side of parlor, where Sheriff Cutler and four of his deputies stood, dark and foreboding in their great coats and black hats. The silver of their badges shown from their lapels. Michael Cutler clearly did not appreciate this display of feminine unity, although several of his deputies were taking the chance to admire the cleavage on display for their perusal.

Sadie took her place next to Opal, who was on the verge of blowing kisses to the deputies. Opal always did enjoy a crowd.

"Heard anything?" Sadie asked in a whisper.

"No," Opal replied out of the corner of her mouth and then she did blow a kiss, aiming squarely at the youngest looking of the deputies. He blushed.

Mistress gazed at her Jewels, seemingly pleased with them. Sadie could tell that Mistress was no less upset than she had been twenty minutes ago. She was merely doing a better job of hiding it.

She turned back to the Sheriff. "We are all assembled, ready for your inspection." She was mocking the man. The cords in his neck tightened and Sadie wondered if this was the wisest course of action, provoking one of the few people who could legitimately arrest them all. "Now why don't you tell me what this is about?"

"Ma'am," Sheriff Cutler began, sounding resigned about the entire situation. "I told you, we only have an arrest warrant for *one* girl. There was no need to drag everyone down here." His gaze was hard, bordering on cruel.

Some of the girls shrank back but Pearl actually took a step forward, as if she were ready to take the lawman on. Of course she would be the one to try. But Mistress raised a hand and Pearl stopped, looking dangerous. The Jewel and the sheriff stared at each other with open animosity.

Mistress's smile glittered. "Really, Michael. Who are you operating under the delusion that you're going to arrest today?" Sheriff Cutler scowled at the use of his Christian name.

Sadie's fingers tangled with Opal's. More than one girl had left a past outside the door when she entered this brothel.

"Sadie Billington. I was told she was here."

She had to breathe. She opened herself to the pain and let it move through her. That name couldn't hurt her.

Mistress was silent for perhaps a moment too long before she said, "Who?"

The air grew heavy with tension. "Give me the girl and there won't be any trouble," Sheriff Cutler said in a menacing voice.

Mistress snorted at this. Delicately. "On whose authority?"

Cutler nodded his head back toward one of the deputies and he stepped forward, holding out a sheet of paper. "The judge's," Cutler went on. "I have a warrant for her arrest. She's wanted on theft in Kentucky. I will bring in this entire establishment if I have to, ma'am."

The Jewels were far too well trained to do

anything like gasp in horror at this blanket threat. In fact, no one made a sound, especially not Sadie. But Opal's fingers tightened around hers. Most of them had probably been arrested at least once, but not here. Arrest meant having your real name revealed. And that often meant going somewhere new to escape the past yet again.

Where would she go? For Mistress was right, this was a safe place for Sadie. She did not want to wind up like that girl in Fort Adams. Like any of the dead girls.

"Perhaps you should check with Free Cyrus Franklin? I hear he takes in criminals," Mistress said as if this were all one giant joke.

But Sadie knew it wasn't. Why was Gerard having her arrested?

Well, it was because she had stolen money so that her sisters might not starve to death. That was not a fact to debate. The bigger question was how had he *known* to have her arrested. No, that question was an insult to his intelligence as well because she'd told him what her name was. He was a smart man and he'd rightly guessed that her safe word was her last name. Somehow, he'd tracked down the Billington family and he probably knew all. Or, almost all, anyway.

"Ma'am," the sheriff said, his voice weary, as if he realized he was on a fool's errand, "Judge Hobson was clear that the girl would be here. And if you're hiding her, that's a crime, too. One I doubt you'd be able to talk your way out of."

This was ridiculous. She gave Opal's fingers a final squeeze for support and then stepped forward. "That won't be necessary, Sheriff. I'm Sadie

Billington. I assure you, Mistress did not know anything about my scandalous past."

Behind the sheriff, at least one deputy snorted, as if there was anything more scandalous than being a whore.

Sheriff Cutler didn't even blink as he unhooked a pair of handcuffs from the belt at his waist. Behind her, the girls gasped in horror, but Sadie only smiled as she held out her wrist. Handcuffs—*this* is something new. Was this part of Gerard's plan?

"That is completely unnecessary," Mistress said, fury undisguised in her voice. "And I will not allow you to take this girl away from me. I will join her."

Sadie turned to look at Mistress, her eyes wide with questions. Gerard wanted to see her, that much was obvious. Her and her alone.

Mistress ignored her. "It is for her own safety."

It was only through years of practice that Sadie managed to keep from rolling her eyes. When had she ever cared for her own safety?

But there was that article in the morning's paper and perhaps Mistress was justified in being nervous. "Fine," she told Mistress as much as she was telling the sheriff. "You may bring both of us to visit the judge."

The sheriff's eyes widened in shock. Clearly, he'd not expected her to start issuing orders. No doubt, he expected her to beg and plead for forgiveness, or protest her innocence.

Her lips twitched. Perhaps that was what the sheriff wanted—but she wasn't going to give it to him.

Reluctantly, the sheriff made his decision. He clipped his handcuffs back to his belt and made a sweeping gesture toward the door. "Shall we, ladies?"

Sadie gave a little curtsy, but she waited for Mistress to move first. And Mistress, it was clear, was not going anywhere without having her say. She made a great show of turning around and surveying her Jewels with loving eyes. "You all know what to do. Serve me well," she said gallantly, as if she were being led off to the gallows instead of barging in on Sadie's arrest.

Like Sadie had said. Ridiculous.

The five men formed a sort of protective circle around Mistress and Sadie as they made their way out of the Jeweled Ladies and down the streets toward the courthouse. In all truthfulness, Sadie did not mind much. After all, there was a killer on the loose.

But underneath that sadness, there was another feeling building as the courthouse came into view. It was Wednesday. She was going to get to see Gerard, on his time.

And it was about time.

Chapter Fourteen

Gerard had always thought that the phrase *sick with worry* was something of a hyperbolic stretch. But as it turned out, he'd never had anything to be this worried about.

Against his will, his eyes kept returning to the newspaper on his desk. Dead girl in Fort Adams. Blonde, slim. His stomach turned at the thought. He was going to be sick if Sheriff Cutler did not show up in the next thirty-seven seconds with Sadie by his side. Because what if she hadn't been at the Jeweled Ladies? What if Mistress had sold her time to someone else? Someone who wouldn't stop?

He tried to reassure himself. There were rules. There had been rules from the very start. Wasn't that why he'd been forced to tolerate Mistress's constant supervision as he learned what he was supposed to do? Because Mistress did not allow her girls to go off alone with men she couldn't trust.

Gerard threw open the door to his office and bellowed at Titus, who was sulking on a bench. Titus had not been allowed to go along for the arrest because he was not a deputy and he was pouting like a five-year-old. "Well?" Gerard roared. "Where the hell are they?"

165

Titus turned his sad puppy dog eyes toward Gerard and shrugged listlessly. He'd come home with no further word from Jack Wyeth and knew he was in trouble.

The delay was bad. The delay meant that they had not been able to find her. No, no—Gerard tried to remind himself that there could be a myriad of reasons as to why it was taking so long for the sheriff to retrieve Sadie. Perhaps she'd been asleep? Perhaps she'd been in the bath. Maybe she'd already left to do her shopping for the day.

It wasn't her. The girl that had been killed? It couldn't be his Sadie. It just couldn't be.

Gerard slammed his door so hard that the frosted glass rattled and he resumed his frantic pacing. Another five minutes—that's how long he would give the sheriff before he went looking for Sadie himself.

But it only took three minutes before the cacophony of boots treading down the hallway filled the courthouse. He had just enough time to pull himself together to start looking like the judge instead of a worried lover before his door banged open and Sheriff Cutler stuck his head in. "We got her, but Mistress insisted on coming. Do you want me to throw her in a cell?"

Gerard ground his teeth together. Why hadn't he accounted for that possibility? Of course Mistress was the reason they took so long to get here. She'd probably been serving Cutler tea in that parlor of hers.

He was getting damnably tired of Mistress's interference. "No, show them in," because he could not wait another moment to see that Sadie was whole and healthy with his own eyes.

And then she was there. She was standing in front of him, uninjured, unblemished. Her flaxen hair had been wound into a simple bun and her dress was one that he recognized as too well made for him to destroy.

All of the worry that had churned his stomach like so much butter melted away at the relief of seeing her. He was barely aware of Mistress stepping in beside her, barely aware of dismissing the sheriff. It was all he could do to hold himself still until the door closed behind the sheriff, cutting the three of them off from the rest of the world.

"Sadie," he breathed in relief, rushing for her and pulling her into his arms. "My God, you have no idea how frantic I've been with worry. Are you all right? Are you unharmed?" As he asked, he moved his hands over her body, watching her face for reaction. He had to feel for himself that she was well.

"Really, Gerard," Mistress said dismissively. "Was this necessary?"

He didn't spare a glance in her direction. But he couldn't resist replying. "I don't recall asking you to be here." Sadie still hadn't said anything. She was holding herself still, her eyes wide as she looked at him. "My dear, are you all right?"

"You had her arrested, Gerard. Do you really have to ask?"

That did it. He was a patient man, but he'd just run out of patience with Mistress. "Do you think you might let her speak for herself? Or is that something that is no longer allowed? I did not ask for you to be here. I am not going to harm her. You do not have to treat her as a child. You may leave and if you do not, I will have you removed. I can think of nothing that would give me greater pleasure than to be rid of your presence, Mistress."

Mistress looked indignant, but he simply didn't care. What he cared about was the gentle sigh that came from Sadie, the way her hand came to rest on his cheek. "It's all right, Gerard," she said. "I gather that you read the article, as well?"

He nodded, leaning into her touch. "I was so worried. I don't—I just—I needed to make sure that wasn't you. I couldn't..." He closed his eyes. "I couldn't face it if something happened to you." He dropped his hands to her waist and pulled her against him. "I don't know how I would go on without you."

It should have been lowering to say that out loud. He was Gerard Hobson and he'd never needed anyone. But that was an old lie, one that he was tired of repeating. And what's more, he didn't have to keep repeating it. Sadie had given him permission to face the truth about who he was and what he wanted out of his meager existence.

Sadie allowed him to hold her. She even rested her head against his shoulder but she did not move her arms around his neck, as she so often did after he'd tended to her. She did not sink into him like she did when he held her on the settee. She held herself apart. Just a little.

"I am well, Gerard. But Mistress is right. You had me arrested."

He held her tighter, willing the words to stop coming out of her mouth.

"How long have you known?"

Irritation scraped over his nerves and it took everything he had to keep his temper. "Can we not have this conversation by ourselves? I have been worried sick about you and I just… I can take care of this. I can fix it. The most important thing is that you are all right."

Then she did something very interesting. She pushed him away. His hands fell uselessly to his sides as he stared at her. "No, you're wrong. The most important thing is that there is a dead girl a mere ten miles away from where we are. The most important thing is that she's probably not the first girl this killer, whoever he is, has murdered. The most important thing is that we find him *now*, before someone else dies by his hand." She looked at Mistress.

Gerard did not pretend to understand the look that passed between the two women, but Mistress nodded in agreement. "She won't like this."

She? She *who*? The only two women whose opinions he remotely valued in matters such as this were already in the room.

"He won't like it, either. None of them will. But it has to be done." There was steel in Sadie's voice that made Gerard smile.

He couldn't keep his hands off her. He picked up her fingers and kissed her knuckles. "You are the strongest woman I have ever met."

She gave him a look that was an open challenge. If they were in the attic of the brothel, he would relish that look, relish the permission it gave him. But he didn't take her up on it. So he sighed and forced himself to be the judge. That's who he was, after all. "What am I not going to like?"

"We need to talk to some people—*you* need to talk to some people. We have our suspicions about who might be doing this."

169

He looked at his Sadie. This was a side of her that he did not get to see in the attic room. There, she submitted to his will and was stronger because of it. But here? Here, she was anything but submissive. She was powerful and righteous. She was... his equal. With a start, he realized that this was quite possibly what true love felt like.

"Who?" he asked dumbly.

Sadie and Mistress shared a glance that seemed worried. Then Sadie heaved a mighty sigh and straightened her shoulders. "You need to talk with Mayor Dupree, Mr. O'Shea, and most especially, Gerard, you need to talk to Emmeline Dupree. Right *now*."

His mouth dropped open as he stared at her. "What?"

"And when you talk to them," Sadie went on as if he hadn't spoken, "you will do so with the utmost respect and propriety. I don't know what has gone on between the three of them and you in the past, but we have a common goal here. You can prove your innocence because you know that people have already started to suspect you for this new crime. Mistress did, until she saw for herself that I was in my room."

He glared at the older woman, who at least had the decency to look ashamed of herself.

"If we are very lucky," Sadie went on, "this is the same man who killed the girl four years ago and you will be completely cleared. But you cannot do that without the help of the Duprees. Do I make myself understood?"

He blinked at her once and then again, but she did not waver at all. "Bossy," he murmured under his breath.

170

She leaned forward then, her body warming his. "This has to be done, Gerard," she whispered in his ear. "Do you agree?"

If they were in the attic, he would put her in her place for issuing such orders and expecting to be followed. But they were not in that attic and, what's more, she was right. He nodded. "I shall have the sheriff fetch them."

"You shall do no such thing," Sadie replied easily, as if she'd been expecting this. "You'll only frighten Mrs. Dupree and that will not help your cause. No, someone whom they know and trust should go and request their presence." She turned Mistress. "If you wouldn't mind."

"And leave you alone with *him*?" She sniffed as if she'd stepped in something foul smelling.

Gerard went to tell Mistress exactly what she could do with her sniffing little nose, but Sadie beat him to the punch. "Yes. Emmeline will need someone she can trust. That someone is *you*."

Who was this ferocious woman standing in his office? It couldn't be the same woman he stripped bare every other Saturday and flogged mercilessly. This woman was a fearsome creature to behold, issuing orders to Mistress, of all people. He'd judged her wrong, he suddenly realized. All of these weeks and months he had not allowed her to kiss him in the privacy of the attic room because he believed that her allegiance lay with Mistress but not with him. But here, tonight? He saw her as she really was. She was Sadie Billington and she was a force to be reckoned with.

Mistress realized it, too. She took a breath that almost sounded like a low growl when she exhaled

171

before she turned her attention back to him. "Gerard," she began.

"Your Honor. In this room, I am Your Honor to you."

She rolled her eyes. *"Your Honor,"* she began again through gritted teeth. "If I bring the Duprees and Hank O'Shea to you will you be able to contain your animosity?"

He looked at Sadie then. Because of her, he'd started to realize that perhaps his hatred of Raymond Dupree had been misplaced all of these years. Because of her, he'd begun to let go of his infatuation with Isabelle Dupree. Because of this woman, he no longer felt like a man who was controlled by demons too dark to even acknowledge.

"Of course. I am only concerned that justice be served."

Mistress sniffed again. "Behave," she said under her breath as she opened the door.

Gerard wasn't sure to whom she was saying it.

The moment the door clicked shut, Gerard pulled Sadie into his arms. "My beautiful girl," he murmured into her hair. "My bossy, brilliant, beautiful girl."

Then and only then did she melt into his arms. "You're going to run out of b-words soon, Gerard."

His heart clenched that she would use his name. Because she could. "Brave," he countered. "Bold."

She made a happy little noise. "I can be all of those things. But it takes a toll on me and then I just want…"

"Someone else to be in charge," he said, leaning back and cupping her face in his hands. "Someone like me."

"Someone exactly like you," she said with a smile. But he thought it looked tinged with sadness in the corners. "We haven't much time. The Duprees will be here soon and I'm under arrest and—"

He kissed her. It wasn't an expert thing because he was no expert. But months of waiting and wanting, of standing aside while she took her pain and pleasure together and denying himself the satisfaction of a release—it all melted away. He'd thought he'd lost her. Lost her without ever giving her the satisfaction of the kiss she so desperately wanted. So he slanted his mouth over hers and set about kissing his Sadie. She tasted sweet, like lemon drops, sunshine and smiles. Her lips were soft and welcoming as they opened for his tender assault. Her arms looped around his waist and he knew she could feel his hardness for her—only for her.

"I want to take you home, tie you to the bedpost and spank you with my bare hands until you scream," he whispered against her lips when he could contain the images in his head no longer.

"And then what?" Her eyes were fluttering and unfocused, the blue darker now.

"And then I want to spread you wide and slide between your legs and have you. I want to have you all to myself, my pet." He would not deny himself this. Not any longer.

She made another happy noise that he swallowed with a second kiss. For a long minute, he explored her mouth. He'd learned so much about her. He knew where to hit her on the backside to leave a mark and how to make her cry. He knew how to touch her with a whip to bring the heights of pleasure and pain.

173

"I want my hands on you, pet. All over you," he murmured against her mouth.

"Gerard." She pushed him away for the second time that night. "We must focus."

"Do you..." he swallowed. "Do you not want that?"

She took a steadying breath. "Of course I do. But we have a problem. Can you control yourself?"

She was right. Of course she was right. "I'm sorry. I'm just so glad to see you."

Her face brightened. "And I, you. Soon, I promise. Soon I will be all yours."

He guided her to a chair in front of his desk and leaned back, still holding her hand in his. "All right. To business. Why do we need the Duprees?"

She fidgeted, but didn't pull her hand away. "Emmeline, Mrs. Dupree, she was attacked some years ago. A man tied her up and nearly beat her to death. Emmeline is *not* like me, it should be noted. Mistress found her and brought her here."

Ah. Perhaps that was part of their problem. The mayor's wife recognized what Gerard was on some level and hated him for it. "Unfortunate. Why is that important now? Are you saying there's a connection?"

This time, she did remove her hand. "About a month ago, she saw that man again, here in Brimstone. She was terrified. We told the mayor and Mr. O'Shea."

He processed this information. "You're saying a violent man known to harm women—against their will," he added, mindful of the distinctions Sadie had taught him, "was spotted in my town and you chose not to tell *me* about it?"

174

Her lips pursed. "Yes. But we did tell Mistress, who warned the other madams. The man left town shortly thereafter."

Some of the happy relief burned away. "Sadie, why didn't you come to me? I'm an officer of the law."

"Because Emmy didn't want anyone to know. As far as we could tell, the man did not recognize her and she didn't want to draw his attention. Gerard, she was *terrified*. You must treat her kindly when she gets here. Mayor Dupree has the political clout to work with Fort Adams and even Beantown to find this man and Mr. O'Shea has the ability to find him or whoever killed that poor girl." She stood and moved closer, resting her hands on his shoulders.

He looked up at her. "This was something you hid from me, Sadie."

She swallowed, looking nervous. "It was."

"And you also hid your history."

That got him an exasperated sigh. "Not that it stopped you. I hope I can be forgiven from hiding a crime from the local judge because look what happened when he found out about it. He had me arrested. *Arrested*, Gerard. Five men sent to bring me in, in front of all my friends."

"I was worried," he said, but he knew it was a poor excuse.

"Then why didn't you come find me? Why did you have to send a posse?"

He pulled her in closer and rested his head against her chest. "I… I panicked. I've known about your theft for weeks now and I—"

"Weeks?" she squeaked.

He nodded, glad he couldn't see the look on her face. "It was badly done of me. Badly done. But I needed you."

"This is a problem, Gerard. I'm a wanted woman. There's a reason we go by false names at the brothel. It would have been bad enough for you to be known associating with Sapphire Bleu the whore but a known thief?" She sighed and stroked his hair. "I shall have to leave town."

"No." He'd just found her. There was no way in hell he could let her go. He *needed* her. Preferably tied to his bedpost and screaming in pleasure.

"At the very least, I shall have to go back to Kentucky and face what I did."

He opened his mouth to argue, but just then, the sound of footfalls filled the hallway outside his office. Reluctantly, he let go of Sadie. "We are not done," he said as he guided her down to the chair.

"I hope not." It wasn't much, those three words, but as the door to his office burst open and admitted Mistress, Dupree, Dupree's wife, O'Shea and the sheriff, Gerard had little choice but to cling to those words.

They weren't done yet.

God, how he hoped.

Chapter Fifteen

Sadie held Emmy's hand as the woman tearfully recounted seeing the man who had harmed her. Mistress and Mr. O'Shea each told what steps they had taken to make sure the man found no quarter in town. The sheriff reported that he'd been in contact with the Fort Adams sheriff, trying to get a full description of the killer thought to be behind this new attack.

The way Sheriff Cutler made this statement without looking anywhere near Gerard only confirmed Sadie's suspicion that the sheriff had been trying to determine if Gerard was behind this killing. She was right. People already suspected him.

"So how do we catch him? If it's the same man—and I thank you for being brave enough to share this information with us, Mrs. Dupree," Gerard said with a nod of his head toward Emmy, which was so civil as to be sincerely polite. "At least we know what he looks like. Even if it's not the same criminal, I don't want that man to harm another woman. Especially not in my town." He cleared his throat and managed to look almost apologetic. "In *this* town," he corrected, nodding to where Mayor Dupree stood behind Emmy's chair.

Gerard didn't so much as glance at Sadie when he said it, but he didn't have to. She knew what he meant.

She fought to keep herself from grinning up at Gerard like a lovesick fool. He'd kissed her. He wanted to put his hands on her. He wanted to consummate their relationship.

He'd also arrested her.

Well, that was inevitable, she supposed. The thing that gave her hope was that he wanted to be with her even though he knew about her unlawful past.

She hadn't seen Gerard in action before, but he was magnificent. He listened, took notes, and most importantly, treated Emmy with all of the respect the mayor's wife deserved. At one point, Sadie caught Mr. O'Shea's eye and lifted her brows. *See?* She thought at him. *He* can *be trusted.*

In response, Mr. O'Shea nodded in her direction. Sadie liked to think that was his way of saying, *you were right.*

"I have an idea," Sadie said after a moment's pause.

All eyes turned to her. "Begging your pardon," Sheriff Cutler began, his voice one step below condescension, "but I'm not even sure why you're part of this conversation, Miss. Aside from you having potentially seen this man, what possible connection do you have to this case?"

Sadie glanced up at Gerard. He didn't smile or wink at her, but something in his eyes changed. "Let's hear what she has to say," he said to the sheriff, without taking his eyes off Sadie

"Yes," said Mistress, "let the girl talk, Michael."

Sadie took a deep breath as Emmy squeezed her fingers. "What if we use me for bait? The dead girl in Fort Adams looked a great deal like me. Perhaps—"

"No," came the resounding shout from nearly everyone in the room. The only person who didn't object was the sheriff.

"Absolutely not," Gerard said at the same time Emmy clutched at Sadie's arm, as if she could physically hold her back from such a rash decision.

"I'm not saying," Sadie went on when they had subsided, "that you all abandon me to whatever sort of monster is out there. But if he's going to be looking for someone in this town, it's going to be me. And I am the only one who could even have a chance of handling him."

"*No*," Gerard repeated again, and the edge in his voice that pushed against Sadie, commanding her obedience. "I won't allow it."

"Why not?" Sheriff Cutler's voice cut through the room like a bullwhip. "She's right. Whoever is cutting up whores is going to be looking for another whore to cut." Sheriff Cutler had clearly judged Sadie for her crimes and found her guilty. Maybe he figured that if she sacrificed herself in so noble a manner, it would make up for stealing the five hundred dollars? "She's just as disposable as any other whore."

No one moved. The whole room was frozen in a sort of awful tableau. Her cheeks heated and she dropped her gaze to her lap. Sadie refused to let what the sheriff had said bother her. She knew this was how it was. She was what she was. But it still stung. Most of the people in the room were as close to her as family. Mistress had trained her and protected her. Emmy was her closest friend. She didn't even think that Mayor Dupree would dismiss her. He'd married Emmy, after all. And Mr. O'Shea… there was a sort of

179

grudging respect there, Sadie thought. And then Gerard...

To these people, she liked to think that she was far more than just a body for men to beat or come on.

Gerard was the one who broke the silence. "I'll thank you to leave this room," he said in a voice that Sadie knew all too well. He was hanging on to the last of his self-control and it was a fight. "Right *now*."

The sheriff snorted. "Don't get your dander up. The girl volunteered, Your Honor."

A quick glance around told her that everyone noticed that Gerard was visibly shaking. Oh, no. If he gave himself over to his anger now it would ruin him more efficiently than she ever would be able to. The sheriff would know he was violent and domineering and any man with eyes would make the connection between Gerard and Sadie.

Suddenly, she was tired—tired of hiding, tired of keeping secrets. But she couldn't let Gerard throw away everything he'd worked for simply because the sheriff had treated her exactly as she was. So she said, "If we don't use me to draw the killer out—"

"And we will not," Gerard interrupted.

She ignored him. "Then what should we do?"

The question hung in the air for a moment before Mr. O'Shea spoke. "Has anyone else talked to Free Cyrus Franklin? The girl from four years ago was dumped at his place. Mayhap there've been other girls that got cut up that found shelter out of his place. We ought to start there."

The sheriff grunted. "And just what do you think he's going to do?"

"More than you've done," O'Shea shot back.

180

"Fine," Gerard interrupted. Even upset, he commanded respect. "I want this man Mrs. Dupree described found. O'Shea, you know his name?"

"Clete Devlin was the name he used at the Golden Star."

He nodded but was silent for a minute. All eyes were on him, so Sadie felt safe in staring at him. This was Gerard in his element, playing a long game against a worthy opponent. "Let's plant a false story," he said decisively. "Instead of using Miss Billington as bait, let's just spread a rumor that she's been injured by this Devlin. I'm willing to bet that being named will draw him out."

"What if it doesn't?" O'Shea asked.

"Then it will drive him farther away and link his name to violence in the press," Mr. Dupree offered.

"No, it *will* flush him out," Gerard said, growing more sure of himself by the moment. "And if he didn't kill that girl, it'll embolden whoever did." He straightened and looked around the room. "It's reasonable to say that the accusations against me made the man who killed that girl four years ago feel confident he could do it again without being caught."

Something in Sadie's chest caught as she watched him talk. Cool, calculating—this wasn't so different from the Gerard she saw in the brothel. But this was who he'd always been—the man he'd never had to hide. This was the man she wanted to know outside of that attic room.

Around the room, people looked contrite. Gerard continued, "Find him. I don't care where he is or how many men it takes. I want him under lock and key, Cutler. O'Shea, talk to Franklin. Mayor Dupree, get the newspapers involved. A believable rumor is a powerful thing. Mistress, continue to press the other madams for information." Miracle of miracles, everyone nodded as they accepted their assignments. Gerard turned to Emmy. "Mrs. Dupree, if we need you to identify the man, we shall be forced to call upon you, but we will all do our best to shield you from this. And Sadie..."

Sadie stared up at him. Did he realize he'd just used her first name? She didn't think so. "Yes?"

Regret touched his eyes. "I cannot allow you to be a part of this manhunt. You are under arrest for theft. Sherriff Cutler, lock her up. But," he went on in an ominous tone, ignoring the gasp of shock from Emmy, "I am charging you with keeping her safe. If anyone—another prisoner *or* one of your deputies—so much as looks at her wrong, heads will roll. Do I make myself clear?"

Mistress raised a stink and Emmy protested vaguely. The mayor and O'Shea began to argue with Gerard, but he ignored everyone and kept his gaze focused on Sadie.

If she contradicted him, what would he do? To change his mind in front of such a loud and vigorous audience would be damaging to his reputation. But Sadie had no desire to be locked up in a cage. This was *not* one of her fantasies.

She couldn't go against him. If he said she needed to be in jail, then she would bow to that demand. She had to believe that this was part of his plan. So instead of adding her voice to the chorus, Sadie just stood and bowed her head to Gerard. "Yes, Your Honor."

Then she turned to where the sheriff was standing, his mouth twisted off into a deep frown.

She and Gerard weren't done. He'd said so himself. However, she didn't see how they were going to finish their conversation, especially not that part where he laid his hands on her, spread her wide and took her, if she were in jail.

Just the thought of that brought a smile to her lips, which made the sheriff scowl even more. "Shall we?"

He rolled his eyes. "Come on."

Sadie paused in the doorway, looking back to where Gerard was a rock in the middle of a storm, calm and collected, staring at her with hunger in his eyes.

No, they weren't done yet.

She just didn't know when they would be.

Soon turned out to be after darkness had fallen over Brimstone. Sadie was sitting in a sparse, relatively clean cell, reading her book. Mistress had sent it and a few other comforts over, including an extra shawl—the midnight blue one Gerard had given her. The deputy on duty wasn't one that Sadie had dealt with much before aside from recognizing him as one of the men who'd come to the Jeweled Ladies that morning. He must have drawn the short straw to get the night shift. Apparently, he'd taken Gerard's warning to heart and was sitting as far away from her side of the jail as possible. No one else was locked up and the room was repressively quiet.

She'd just tucked the shawl around her shoulders more tightly when the door to the jail banged open.

She jumped. "Lemmons," Gerard said, striding into the room with all the authority he possessed. "Miss Billington is being released to my care."

"Your Honor," Lemmons squeaked, almost falling out of his chair. His playing cards flew everywhere. "Who?"

Gerard favored the deputy with a dull look. He didn't so much as glance in Sadie's direction. "The *girl*, Lemmons. The only one in custody. She's being released."

"But I thought she had a warrant?" Lemmons had managed to find his feet and was trying to tuck in his shirt as he spoke.

"She does," Gerard said with forced patience. Sadie stood, but he didn't acknowledge her. He brandished a piece of paper. "It's all in order. All you need to do is unlock the cell."

Lemmons' mouth opened and shut a few times.

"Now," Gerard said, menace bleeding into his tone.

"Yes, sir. I mean, Your Honor, sir." He fumbled for the ring of keys that was tucked next to the gun cabinet behind the sheriff's desk.

Gerard took a wearying breath but Sadie had to cover her mouth to hide her grin. He really was an imposing man, in perfect command. Again, she found herself wondering if he was even aware he did it or if it came as naturally to him as breathing.

She stood back and quickly gathered her few belongings—her book, her reticule and the small basket of provisions Della had packed for her.

Lemmons was trying to hurry under Gerard's watchful eye but that was only making him clumsy.

He dropped the keys and then tripped over a chair leg on his way to her cell door, barely catching himself before he went sprawling. "Sorry, Your Honor, sir," he mumbled, turning an interesting shade of pink.

"Just get on with it, man. I don't have all night to stand here and watch you bumble about."

After Lemmons successfully made it to her cell door, it took two false starts before he got it unlocked. He went to grab her by the arm to drag her out of the cell, but Gerard said in a quiet voice that carried nonetheless, "I wouldn't touch her, if I were you."

The deputy's hand dropped as if he'd realized Sadie were burning. "Of course not, sir. I mean…"

"Oh, do shut up." Gerard stepped forward, a harsh glint in his eyes. "Come with me."

She inclined her head and stepped free of the cell. What was he about? But she didn't dare say anything else with Lemmons listening.

"Do you need to bind her hands?" Lemmons asked after them as they made their way silently toward the door.

Gerard froze, his back stiff. Really, it shouldn't be this hard to keep from smiling, Sadie thought.

"Why would I need to do that?" he asked carefully.

"Because she might escape," Lemmons offered in a weak voice. "She's a wanted woman, sir. I mean…"

Gerard didn't bother to dignify this with a response. Instead, he took Sadie firmly by the elbow and led her out of the jail, Lemmons sputtering in confusion behind them.

Once outside, he slid his grip on her elbow down so that her hand was tucked against his arm. They

185

walked on for some time. He was moving quickly and she had to lengthen her stride to keep up with him. "Is this a jail break?" she finally asked as they moved away from Main Street and toward a dark row of houses.

"Good Lord, no."

"I wasn't sure. I've never had an officer of the court get me released before."

"You're under arrest. You've been released into my care. I'm completely responsible for you." He glanced at her out of the corner of his eye. The harshness was gone and in its place was something else—something that warmed Sadie against the cold cut of the wind.

"Indeed," she murmured.

"The paper is going to press in the morning with rumors of your demise. It's best if you weren't discovered in the jail when the paper hits."

She considered this. He was going to hide her away. "Ah. So this is a tactical retreat?"

"Indeed. Mistress wanted me to tell you that she's assured the other girls you're in fine health."

"Are you taking me back to the brothel?" She could hide in the attic room quite comfortably.

"No," came the short reply. In fact, they were going in the opposite direction.

Long minutes passed as she enjoyed the luxury of walking on Gerard's arm in public. True, it was dark out and the wind kept all but the most insistent of people indoors. But she was on his arm, walking through town. They weren't hiding. It felt deeply, profoundly *normal*.

It was the sort of thing she wanted and exactly the

sort of thing she didn't allow herself to dream of. But wouldn't it be something if she could be his lady, parading through town with her head held high and her well-earned bruises hidden?

She pushed the image away. These things, marriage and respectability, they weren't for her. Not with this man, especially. No, she was a whore and a criminal. No matter how much he might care for her, and today had made it clear that he did, he wouldn't be able to get past the blow to his reputation by associating with her in the bright light of day. So she contented herself with this, silently strolling the streets, his arm under hers. This would be a memory she'd treasure in the coming weeks and months, the now-inevitable trip back to Kentucky, the trial, facing her sisters and having her life as Sapphire Bleu permanently marring their chances.

A gust of wind hit her face and she closed her eyes against it, against all of it.

He led her past the Dupree mansion, where the only light was in an upstairs window. Sadie spared a thought for Emmy. Hopefully, the morning hadn't been too trying for her.

Then Gerard whisked her farther down the street toward the Hobson house. It wasn't as grand as the Dupree mansion, but it was a good two stories tall. It fit a man like Gerard, she decided as they approached.

Silently, Gerard led her up the front steps. He unlocked the door and handed her in. The rooms smelled of cigar smoke and... paper. Like there were a great many books in this house, all waiting to be read. It was so perfectly Gerard. No one else had quite the same scent he did.

187

He stepped in behind her and shut the door against the wind. For a moment, they stood in the dark, neither moving nor speaking. Then Sadie turned to him just as he stepped into her and their mouths found each other as if by silent agreement and he was kissing her. There was no hesitation, no debate about the rightness or wrongness of it all. No lectures on morality or discussion of lines he couldn't cross. There was just this true, undisguised passion. His mouth was rough against hers, the stubble on his chin scraped along her cheek. She shivered as he kissed her hard enough to bend her over backwards.

For months, she'd been surrendering everything she had to him. Now, it was her turn to take what she wanted.

She opened to him and nipped at his lower lip, drawing him deeper into the kiss as his arms came around her waist and clutched her to his chest. As he did so, she let her hands explore over his body. For so long, she hadn't been allowed to touch him, except afterwards, when he consented to her arms around his neck.

That changed now. She undid the buttons on his coat and slid it from his shoulders, letting her hands follow the muscles of his arms down. She loved the feel of rope on her wrists, but his body under her hands was better. She wanted to touch all of him. She didn't know when she'd get another chance.

He was hot against her, his cock growing harder as he dug his fingers into her hips and pulled her against him. But he didn't move to undress her. Instead, he submitted to her inspection.

The buttons on his waistcoat gave and it, too,

went sliding to the floor. She'd known that he was not a weak man. Weak men did not leave her marked like he did, but she'd only dreamed of how he was built. He wasn't muscular, not overly so. There was a leanness to his build that she found pleasing. And although he had long since gone gray, his body hadn't gone soft. She ran her hands over the fine linen of his shirt, feeling the muscles of his chest, which finally made him break the kiss.

"Sadie…" he moaned.

Surrender, she thought. Finally, this was a man who was going to completely surrender to her.

"Take me to bed, Gerard."

It was *not* a request.

Chapter Sixteen

Everything about Gerard stilled as Sadie's words hung in the air around them. Finally, after all this time, he had her alone and she was issuing orders?

The darkness of his hall was close around them, safe. In that darkness, he smiled. This woman. God, this woman.

He swept her feet out from under her and cradled her in his arms. She let out a little squeak of surprise as he moved to the stairs. "How are you?" he asked, nuzzling her hair with his nose. She smelled only faintly of the jail, but he didn't have the patience to draw her a bath and wash her first.

"Still sore," she replied, shifting in his arms. His left arm was across her back, where she most likely still sported an impressive collection of bruises from his last flogging. "But I don't care. I just want your hands on me."

"God, yes." He carried her down the hall to his room.

It was small. Gerard's father hadn't wanted to waste money on anything so earthly as a grand house, so nothing was bigger than it needed to be. Gerard could only hope that Sadie didn't mind the close quarters.

Cozy, he thought to himself as he kicked open the door and carried her into the bedroom. He hoped that she thought it was cozy. The bed was big enough for his frame, but it wasn't a massive four-poster bed or anything like that. However, it did have a turned wooden headboard and that was all he needed.

He sat her down on the mattress and stood over her for a moment, untying the strings of her bonnet and then smoothing her blonde hair away from her cheeks. She submitted to these tender caresses, her chest heaving. That made him feel good. His kisses hadn't left her unaffected.

He wanted to go slow and show her how good he could be for her. He wanted to rip that dress off her and take her hard, right now. He wanted to lavish attention on her and he wanted to bury himself in her and he wanted to set his hands to her delicate skin and make her beg for it—for him.

The confusing swirl of contradicting thoughts brought him up short. He didn't know what he was doing. The last time he'd tried, it had ended horribly. Doubt crept in, insidious and mean.

What if he couldn't be what she needed?

The thought alone was ridiculous. She may want him, but she didn't *need* him. Surely she'd other, better lovers. In fact, by morning's light, she would recall that he'd arrested her and revealed her name to the town at large.

"You're shaking," she said, taking his hand in hers and pressing it to her cheek.

"I just—I mean—" He cleared his throat and tried again. "Are you sure? About this?" *About me?* Because he wasn't.

191

"Light a candle, Gerard." Her voice was soft, but that steel he'd heard earlier was still there. "I want you to see how much I want you."

Something in his chest unclenched. "Bossy," he said, patting her cheek and then setting about to do as she asked.

"May I ask you a question?"

"Of course." The candle flared and caught.

"Have you ever done this before? Bedded a woman?"

Gerard decided that he preferred *bedded* to *fucked*. "No." If it were anyone else, he would deny it. There was no pride in being a fifty-two-year-old virgin. He set the taper on the small bedside table and turned back to her.

"Are you nervous?"

Oh, it was so hard to admit to it. But he didn't want to hide from her. Not her. "A little. I don't want you to be..." he waved his hands in the air. "Disappointed," he finally finished. "In me."

She tilted her head to one side, considering. "It's much like learning how to dominate me, Gerard. I would be a fool to expect perfection on your first time. No," she went on before disappointment could set its hooks into his chest, "all I want is to be with you."

"Will you..." he swallowed. To ask for assistance went against his nature. "Will you tell me what to do?"

She stood then, her breasts brushing against his chest as his arms came around her. "I think," she said, and her voice was deeper now, more sensual, "that you've thought about this moment for such a long time that you will need very little direction." She leaned up on her tiptoes and pressed kisses along his jaw as her fingers went to the buttons on his shirt. "Tell me how you've imagined us together."

She tugged at his tie, but it didn't budge. He set her back and undid the pin, dropping it next to the candle. "This… this is good," he said when she pulled the scrap of silk from his neck. "You undressing me like this. It's good."

She made a humming noise in the back of her throat as she made quick work of his buttons. Slowly, she pushed the linen from his shoulders, revealing his bare chest. "I've wondered about this," she said. "Is it all right if I taste you here?" A single fingertip traced a path down his chest and around a flat nipple.

"Yes." His voice broke like a schoolboy's as she leaned forward and set her lips to him. Instantly, he was hard again, throbbing for her.

"Tell me what else you've thought about," she murmured against his skin as her hands drifted lower over his stomach.

"I…" He swallowed. Her fingers had found his trouser buttons. "I have so many thoughts. I don't know. Do you want them in order?" The last part came out as a squeak because her hand had brushed against his cock and he almost lost control right then and there.

Sadie rested her cheek against his stomach and looked up at him. "Touch me, Gerard," she commanded and he was helpless to resist her because that was what he wanted.

Was this how it was for her, too? Maybe it was, he decided as he set his hands to her hair and pulled the prim bun loose. "I'm going to muss your hair up."

"I would be sad if you didn't," came the sultry

193

reply as she pushed his trousers down over his hips and set to work on the strings of his drawers. "That may be one of my favorite times with you, when you brush my hair."

"Really?"

"It's not so much the hair," she explained, pushing his drawers down. "It's you taking care of me. I do so love it when you take care of me, Gerard."

He sprang free, the cold air a shock against his skin. As she studied him, doubt tried to elbow its way back into this room. He had no points of comparison, but she did. Was he too big? Not big enough? Was he even normal? Well. That thought made him almost laugh. He'd spent months striping her skin. *Normal* wasn't the right word for it.

Her bun tilted to the side as she leaned against his waist. Slowly, she lifted one hand and stroked his length. "Do you think about me touching you like this?"

His eyes tried their damnedest to flutter shut as a world of sensation concentrated about his cock, where her fingers slid over his shaft, the tip. But he wasn't going to miss a moment of this. "In... in my thoughts, I'm not so..." So timid, so nervous.

"Do you grab me by my hair and thrust into my mouth?" Her fingers closed around his length and she stroked, her grip firm.

He almost lost it right then and there. He had to hold onto her hair to keep from buckling over and pinning her beneath him on the bed. "I... yes."

"Do you tie me to the bed and spank me until I'm begging for release?" she asked, her tone knowing as she stroked up, down, up again.

194

"Yes." He shuddered under her touch and the assault of images she gave voice to.

"And when I beg and plead, Your Honor, do you tie my legs open and drive this handsome cock up into me until you're sheathed to the hilt inside of my pussy?" Her other hand slid up between his legs and she fondled his jewels. "Until I'm thrashing underneath you, so wild with desire that you have to hold me down?"

"Sadie—*please*," he whimpered. *Handsome.* Who knew a cock could be such a thing?

"Or," she went on, ignoring his need as she continued to admire him, "do you bend me over the bed and smack my ass as you fuck me so hard? Do you cry out my name when you come?" She squeezed. *Everywhere.*

His world narrowed to her hands on his body. This was exactly why he hadn't allowed her to touch him before now. Because he couldn't do anything but surrender to his desires.

"We have all night," she assured him as she kissed him on the stomach, a sweet touch. "You may do as you wish with me, sir."

Maybe it was the kiss, maybe it was the *sir*—whatever it was, he surrendered. Completely and totally. For the first time in his life, he gave himself up to passion.

He jerked her head back. "What?"

A shiver went through her as her eyes widened knowingly. She looked very much like a woman who had just come away from a battle of the wills victorious and he was the prize.

"*Sir*," she said, throwing the challenge back in his face.

195

He slapped her cheek and then grabbed her face. She moaned, a sound he knew all too well. "Your Honor," she whispered.

They were alone. He was going to have sex with her. This was glorious.

He dragged her face to his cock. "Suck," he ordered.

She wrapped her hand around his shaft again, but he hauled her hands away and pinned both of her wrists against his chest. Then, with his other hand, he guided her head back to his cock. "Just your mouth."

He watched in fascination as her lips pursed, as she let him guide her head so that her lips were pressed against his tip. Then he pushed against her mouth and she opened and he slid into her warm wetness.

"Oh my God," he groaned. His hips began to move of their own volition as he surrendered to her.

And Sadie? She did what she always did. She took what he gave her willingly. Happily, even. He held fast to her wrists and pumped into her mouth and he did not hold back. They had all night. Maybe, depending on how things went down in the press, maybe they had several nights.

God, maybe he could keep her.

She shifted on the bed. He should have stripped her out of her serviceable wool dress before, but there was something about her looking so prim and proper as her mouth worked him over—

"I want to let go," he got out through gritted teeth. "I *need* to." God, he hadn't needed anything so much in his life.

She looked up at him, her mouth still sucking on his cock, and nodded as her fingers flattened against

196

his chest. She hummed and the noise went straight through him.

"*Beautiful—girl.*" It was all he could say, think, see and feel as he exploded into her mouth. There was no dignity in it, no respectability. There was nothing moral or ethical about this, about any of it. He didn't care. She sucked at him as he finished and went soft. When his strength failed him and he started to sway, she pulled her wrists free and wrapped them around his waist, holding him up even as her mouth gentled on him.

When she finally broke the contact, shame tried to skirt in. He should have taken care of her first. She deserved so much more than that. She deserved *everything*.

"Your Honor," she said in a soft voice, looking up at him with soft eyes. She licked her lips, tasting every last bit of him.

"Sadie," he said, trying to get the ground back underneath his feet. "I didn't—I mean, I should have—"

Her brows knit together. "Was I not good, Your Honor?"

Oh, God. He was messing this up. He stroked her cheek and forced himself to breath. "You were. It was... amazing. But I need to take care of you, too. You should come first. You should always come first."

Ah, that was the right thing to say because her whole face lit up. "You have let me come so many times, Your Honor." She drew little circles on his stomach that sent small ripples of warmth through his body. "It was your turn. I've wanted to do that for *so* long."

197

"Really?" He wanted to believe that, he did. But he wasn't sure he could.

She nodded, so earnest. "I can take so much more, Your Honor. I can take everything you want to give me."

He ran a hand under her chin and lifted her so that she wasn't sheltered against his body anymore. Did she know what she was saying? Because he was in love with her. Maybe he'd been for a long time. All those months of secret meetings in a hidden room had forged a bond between them. But after watching her take command this morning when, by rights, she should have been scared or hysterical? After seeing her calmly reading in the cell he'd put her in? After watching her swallow him down and ask if she'd been good?

"Everything?" He bent over and brushed his lips against hers. Did she taste like him? The idea thrilled him. "Even if I want to make you mine?"

"I'm already yours," she whispered, her mouth moving against his. "I want it *all*."

He smiled. The world had righted itself and the ground underneath his feet was firm again. "Then that's exactly what you're going to get."

Chapter Seventeen

A shiver of anticipation ran through her as Gerard kicked out of his boots and pants. "Really, Gerard, you kept this hidden from me?" she asked, reaching out to stroke a hand down his chest.

He smacked her hand away. "I had to be sure." He stood her up and began to work at the buttons on her dress. "How much do you value your shift today?"

"Hmm. I don't have another one with me, so maybe we could wait on destroying it for now? Unless you're planning on returning me to the Jeweled Ladies in the morning."

"We'll have to leave the shift in one piece, then," he said, sounding petulant. But he grinned when he said it.

That grin took her breath away. She wasn't just here for the night. How long could she hide here, indulging in the fantasy of living with Gerard? "Have I ever told you how handsome you are when you smile?"

He snorted as the buttons gave way. "I'm not, you know."

"Don't be ridiculous. You are unfairly handsome." He pushed the dress off her shoulders and freed her arms. She took advantage and grabbed at his half-hard cock.

"Hey!" he yelped, surprised. "Oh, no you don't."

He spun her around and worked the dress off her hips. She stepped clear of it and allowed him to pull it away. But then she turned and grabbed at him again. Slightly more than half-hard this time.

For a man of his years, he was making an impressive showing.

"Stop that," he growled, turning her back around so he could unfasten her corset. When that, too, had been cast aside, she felt the shift tighten at her neck and she knew he wanted to rip it off her, but common sense won out and he lifted it over her head.

"Stockings?" she asked, reaching for him again.

"Leave them on." He captured her hands just as she closed her fingers around his cock. "Bossy," he sighed, but it was a happy noise. He was happy. It was such a wondrous thing that it took everything she had not to throw herself at him.

"What are you going to do about it? By my count, we've only just gotten started."

He slapped her ass.

"Sir," she said cheekily, her bottom stinging.

"Oh, that's it. You're asking for it, aren't you?"

She was. But he produced a short length of rope from the bedside table and bound her wrists. Then he pushed her back onto the bed.

He was still in control of himself as he produced a second piece of rope and used that to tie her to the headboard, leaving her enough room to roll over. He positioned her in the middle of the bed, his gaze sweeping up and down her body before he notched an eyebrow at her. "I'm waiting."

She laughed. This was so much more relaxed than

their time in the attic had been. There, he'd wanted her, but he hadn't allowed himself to take everything he wanted. Her heart ached for him, for all the times he'd held himself back on principle.

Principles were a lonely way to live.

This was more. It was comfortable and easy and fun. "Keep waiting," she teased, knowing full well what such insolence would get her.

He bit his lip, his cock twitching between them. "Do you consent?"

"I do."

That was all it took. He slapped her breast and then grabbed her and flipped her over. "You do *what*?"

She fought back the moan. "*Sir*. I do, Sir."

She waited for the first blow, but it didn't come. Instead, she felt his warm lips upon her back, which was still healing from their session on Saturday. "My brave girl," he murmured. "You take all this for me, do you?"

Sadie sighed at the touch. "Everything for you, Gerard."

"That's not the right answer, pet." He began to spank her. He'd hit her so many times, but aside from occasionally slapping her face, he'd never laid a hand on her. Whips, rope—but never just his hand.

Every time his skin connected with hers, her body tensed. The reaction was involuntary and the ache between her legs, the ache that had started when he'd thrust into her mouth, began to build.

A particularly stinging blow had her crying as she tried to twist away from him. Then, the next thing she knew, he'd slipped his hand up between her legs and was actually stroking her pussy.

201

"Oh, Gerard," she said as his fingers slid over the wet folds of her flesh.

"So long," he said, his voice reverent. "I've been watching you do this to yourself for so long and it's been killing me to stand aside. You're the most beautiful woman I've ever known and watching you stroke yourself is the most sensual thing I've ever seen."

She scooted her legs apart. "Do you want to be inside me?" Because that's where she wanted him.

His fingers stilled against her. "Is it all right?"

"*Please.*"

He rubbed against her slit for a moment and then one finger tentatively slid into her. "Oh, God," she moaned, writhing against his hand. "More."

His hand closed around the back of her neck. "Stop squirming," he ordered as he held her down and made his exploration of her.

He was an excellent student, listening for her gasps of pleasure and backing off when she shook her head no. After a few minutes of leisurely touching, Sadie was panting, already close. She'd waited for this for *so* long...

And then he withdrew his hand. She groaned in disappointment but he cut her off with another swat on her bottom. "Keep complaining," he told her between blows, "and you'll really get it."

Her bottom was burning when he stopped and flipped her over. "God, Sadie," he groaned as he cupped her sex, trying to find the spot where she'd touched herself so many times for him. "Here?"

"Down... down... yes," she breathed as his fingers found the right spot.

202

"And is this okay?" He covered her breast with his hand and began pulling on her nipple, rubbing the tip between his finger and thumb.

"Gerard!" Her body bucked as his attentions focused on those small touches.

He chuckled. "I'll take that as a *yes*."

Again, he brought her up to the edge of her crisis and again, he left her there.

"You're going to drive me mad," she panted.

"I learned from the best."

That was when she remembered telling him that the masters, like Mistress, could bring her to the edge repeatedly. He was simply doing what she'd told him to do.

"Gerard—"

He slapped her tit.

She yelped at the spike of pain. God, it felt so good. "Your Honor," she said again, trying to slid her hips toward him. "I need you."

"So bossy."

"You like me like that," she retorted, lifting her leg and trying to wrap it around him.

With a wicked smile on his face, he grabbed her leg, pinned it to the bed and slapped her sex. Not hard, but enough that the shock waves tore through her body. All those lessons were paying dividends right now. He was in complete control, holding her at the edge of oblivion, a viciously sweet smile on his face as he laid his hands all over her body.

"Please, please," she begged, her nipples stinging, her pussy throbbing. "Oh, please, Your Honor. I've been so good."

"Shh," he said, lowering his mouth and suckling

her breast. Then he added teeth and she spiraled out of control again, straining against him. "Not yet. Soon."

She tried to keep quiet, but she couldn't keep still. She couldn't think of anything but where he bit her, where he kissed the pain away, where he stroked and tapped her. The rope ate at her wrists but she couldn't stop moving against him. She was nothing more than his plaything, a creature of sheer passion. Everything, for him.

Then, suddenly, he pulled back and climbed between her legs. "My love," he said, grabbing her by the hips and sliding her to where he wanted her.

"Yes, yes," she whimpered as he pressed the tip of his cock against her. "Like that. Just like that, Gerard."

"Shut up," he said, although his tone was gentle compared to his words. He put a hand on her throat to hold her down and then, in one thrust, he buried himself in her. "Now, pet," he whispered hoarsely. "I want to feel you come around me."

Sadie shattered on command, her body pulsing around his. Gerard groaned as he fell forward onto her. "Oh, God, Sadie. My beautiful Sadie."

He began to thrust into her, filling the hollow ache that had haunted her for months on end now. Nothing mattered but this passion and trust between them. He had her by the throat, tied to his bed and she would give him more, if she could.

A second climax tore through her, lifting her hips off the bed. Gerard shuddered into her, but he did so silently. Sadie smiled to herself. Of course he did.

He collapsed onto her, both of them breathing hard. His hand left her throat and then he was untying her wrists, kissing the rope burns there, curling her into his arms and whispering, "Such a good girl. My brave, beautiful girl."

"You're stuck on the Bs again, Gerard," she managed to murmur against his throat.

He laughed and kissed her. "Was that good, my love?"

His love. "Wonderful."

He rolled onto his back, pulling the covers up over them. "I was trying to avoid the bruises."

"Trust me, the bruises are the last thing I'm thinking about right now." He chuckled again. "Are you happy, Gerard? Did I make you happy?" She was sure she had, but she wanted him to say it.

"Very much so, pet. Oh." He put her aside and climbed out of bed, returning with a wet cloth. Slowly, he cleaned her and then he brought some salve and tended to her wrists. "Let me brush your hair."

She was drowsy with satisfaction, but she sat up for him and let him finish taking care of her. "How long do we have?" she asked around a yawn.

"A few days, maybe. Mistress agreed you should stay here until we flush out Devlin."

A few days. "And then I'll go to Kentucky?"

The brush paused. "I am afraid so, my dear."

She nodded. "Does it matter if the money kept my sisters from whoring?"

"It matters to me. But not to the law." He sat the brush aside and pulled her down under the covers again. "I'll take care of it, though. It's the least I can do."

"How?" she yawned again.

"Shh. Go to sleep now, my love."

She snugged in deeper. "I'll need some things. Another shift, at least."

"Shh," he whispered again, kissing her shoulder. "It's all taken care of. Sleep."

His arms were warm around her waist. One hand cradled her breast. Such a short time to taste the kind of happiness that she didn't deserve. She sank into sleep, warm and happy and safe in his arms, one thought on her mind. "I love you, too."

Chapter Eighteen

She loved him.

Gerard settled disputes and issued fines as the head of the court in Brimstone and the surrounding county.

And she loved him.

He met with Sheriff Cutler and Mayor Dupree. He ignored the whispers that seemed to follow him everywhere, blaming him for the disappearance of Sapphire Bleu.

Because she loved him.

"You seem quite well," Mistress said, removing her black hat with matching veil and setting it on the chair next to her.

Of course, he was well. Sadie loved him.

The ridiculous woman was dressed in ridiculous widow weeds. Honestly, Gerard thought she was playing this mourning a bit too much. But that was part of their cover. Mistress did not know where her Sapphire was and she was acting as if the girl had come to a most foul end.

Not that he wanted to admit why he was so happy to Mistress, of all people. No doubt, she didn't know the meaning of the word. So he pretended she hadn't said anything.

"Have you heard anything from the madam in Beantown?" That was a key part of his plan, getting the madam who claimed that a man looking very much like Gerard had killed her girl four years ago to recant that statement.

Mistress gave him a long look, the kind of long look that made Gerard nervous. "I may have something for you. She claims that she was given a sum of twenty dollars and a list of descriptions and told to speak to a reporter. She has no memory of any man from four years ago."

Because there were so many. Neither of them said that out loud, however. "And will she testify in court as to who paid her to say that?"

"That depends on whether or not you would charge her with a crime."

How had he come to this place in his life, where he hid a prostitute in his house? Where the madam of a brothel was perhaps his most valuable contact? Where he was considering offering immunity to a different madam?

Well, he knew. Sadie loved him. She was no longer just a whore. She was a woman. Perhaps a complicated one, but a woman nonetheless. And to her, Gerard was nothing more than a man. Not a monster, not a demon and most certainly not a killer. Just a man.

A man she loved.

"As she has not made such statements under oath, she has not committed perjury. Therefore, I don't see a need to charge her with a crime." He willfully overlooked the fact that she'd been paid money to make false statements.

Mistress looked pleased. "Any word on our killer?"

"The last report I had, he'd been sighted in Rio Rojo." Running for the border like a coward.

"Madame Clarissa at Fort Adams confirmed the missing tooth. We may never know who killed the girl four years ago, though. Can you live with that?"

Gerard stared at her. "They'll bring him back alive. They have their orders."

Mistress gave him one of those knowing smirks that he hated. "And here I thought you had a better understanding of the common criminal. Cowards like that will never willingly face what they've done. Now," she went on, before Gerard could respond. "How is Sadie today?"

He commanded his skin not to flush. Before he'd left her this morning, he'd stroked over the sensitive skin of her sex until she was begging for release. And then, feeling happy and cruel, he'd told her that she was not allowed to let go until he returned that night, well after dark. The sound of her agonized moans still echoed through his mind. All day long, she would be miserably on edge, waiting for him to come home and take care of her. And she would wait, because she loved him.

"She is well." Mistress did not need to know what went on between him and Sadie in private.

"Domesticity suits you, Gerard."

He stiffened at the statement. This was not domesticity. This was nothing more than playacting. And no matter how wonderful it was, it would not last.

The thought made him unexpectedly sad. And sadness was not an emotion he enjoyed.

Then he realized something. "You called her Sadie, not Sapphire."

Mistress stood and affixed her hat back to her hair. "Haven't you read the newspaper? Sapphire Bleu is dead. I, for one, do not think that she will be resurrected."

Something else bothered him. "You haven't requested payment for her time with me this week."

The look in her eyes was almost pitying. Gerard hated it.

"My dear man," she said with a heavy sigh. "She is no longer under my protection. Surely, after all of this time, you have realized that I was never in control of her. Sadie is as she always has been—a young woman who is doing exactly what she wants."

How did that make any sense? "What do you mean?"

"This is the final lesson I have to teach you, Gerard. You may tie her up and flog her. You may make love to her. She may be at your mercy. But the truth is, she is the one who is in control. Always. We bend to her wishes, not the other way around."

His head began to spin. What was she saying? "A deputy from Kentucky will be arriving any day now to take her back. She'll have to stand trial for her crime." That was his fault. Oh, not the crime. He knew he could not claim responsibility for that. But that little piece of the past would have stayed safely buried if it hadn't been for him. "I can't keep her."

He wished he could. God, how he wished there was a way.

Mistress turned toward the door, but stopped before she opened it. "You're an intelligent man,

Gerard. You've been a worthy opponent but I think now you're a better…"

"Do not say *friend*," he said, grimacing. He could stomach much in this life, but calling one of the most notorious madams a friend was stretching it.

"Ally, then," she agreed with a small smile. "I should think that if there was something you truly wanted, you would find a way to get it. After all, if Sadie can do it, can't you?"

*

There had been a time when the hardest thing he'd ever done in his life had been watching Isabelle run from him. To watch her marry another man and give birth to a son that should've been his and wasn't.

What a fool he'd been.

Because now he knew better. That had been terrible, yes. But not worth the weight he'd given it. And it was nothing compared to how difficult it was to stand aside as Mistress came to fetch Sadie. The plan was that they were not going to acknowledge that Sadie had spent six glorious, perfect nights under his roof and in his bed. Instead, they were going to claim that Sadie had spent that time hidden away in the attic, fearing for her life. It was a good plan, solid and sound.

All he had to do was let her go.

It got harder the next morning, when a Pinkerton agent showed up to transport Sadie back to Kentucky. Because they needed to prove to the town that Sadie was alive and well, the girl was paraded down the street. He watched the whole thing from the window of his office.

211

Harder still was watching none other than Hank O'Shea saddle up alongside Sadie and the Pinkerton agent. They couldn't spare an officer of the law from Brimstone. Most of them were still tracking down Devlin somewhere near the border with Mexico. So Gerard had been forced to ask O'Shea to accompany Sadie. He didn't like O'Shea, but he had to trust him in this situation. The man would make sure that Sadie got back to Lexington whole and healthy.

As they rode out of town, Sadie looked back over her shoulder. Gerard desperately wanted to think that she was looking at him. He put his hand on the glass and watched as his heart rode away.

He stood at his window long after they had ridden out of view. He'd spent last night alone in his own bed, which now smelled of Sadie. He'd felt the ghost of her touch against his cheek, the warmth of her body in his arms. But it was all an illusion because she was gone.

He was trying to make sense of all of it. Anger spiked through him. Why had she stolen the money? If she'd only followed the rules they wouldn't be in this awful position now. But that anger was short-lived as Mistress's words came back to him. Sadie was a young woman who did exactly what she wanted.

She could've married that man, Wyeth. If not him, then someone else. That would've provided protection for her family and kept her sisters off their backs. But then she would've been bound to someone who saw her as a delicate, fragile young woman in need of protection from the slings and arrows of outrageous fortune.

Sadie had told him once that she was glad that Isabelle hadn't married him. They would've made each other miserable. No doubt she'd realized the same thing much, much sooner than Gerard had. If she'd married that man, she would've spent her life knowing that there was something missing and never finding satisfaction. Instead, she'd done what she wanted. She'd protected her sisters. She'd chased her pleasure. And as for him... she'd said she loved him. He desperately wanted to believe that. He didn't want to think that they had confused acceptance with affection. He didn't want to think about her telling her other customers that she loved them.

There had to be a way. If she was going to refuse him, he wanted her to be the one to tell him.

This was the point he'd come to in his life. Everything he'd valued for years and years—morality, his code of ethics, the rule of law—he was willing to put it all aside for one woman. A woman who single-handedly undermined every belief he'd stood for. A whore, a criminal.

No. She may be those things, but they did not define her. She was Sadie Billington. She knew who she was and she knew what she wanted and she let no one—not even him—stand between her and her heart's desires.

He smiled as a plan began to take shape in his mind. After all, he was Judge Gerard Hobson. He was an officer of the law. He ran this town—or tried to, anyway. But those things didn't define him, either. Because now he knew who he was. He was a man with dark tastes and a powerful need to hold on to the happiness that had graced his life for a short time.

He was in love with Sadie Billington and by God, nothing was going to get in his way of telling her just that.

Chapter Nineteen

The odd thing about this return to Lexington after so many years away was how *not* odd it felt. The city had changed since Sadie had abandoned it, but it didn't inspire any sorrow in her. How could she be sad about something that she'd never really missed?

By the time her mother had delivered Daisy, the fourth Billington daughter, she could barely get out of bed. At the age of six, Sadie found herself taking care of her sisters and her mother. The two babies after that killed her mother. And for what? All because her father loved her so much that he couldn't keep his hands to himself? He couldn't be bothered to take a single precaution to prevent pregnancy?

Sadie had been having all kinds of sex with all kinds of men for years now and had never once gotten pregnant because she took precautions.

Her father had drank himself to death after her mother had died because he claimed he couldn't live without his wife. But if that were true, why had he been the one to slowly and inexorably lead her toward the grave with all of those babies?

Sadie had spent ten years trying to hold the family together. Lexington was not a thing to be missed, but a reminder of her success and her failure.

She'd preserved her sisters, but not the Billington family name.

In her absence, her sisters had grown up. They all came to see her in the women's section of the jail, bringing her books and food and trying to look brave and mostly failing, miserably.

May was a schoolteacher and engaged to a pastor. Lucy had a job at a jeweler's store and was engaged to a Jewish man. Daisy was finishing her studies to become a nurse and spoke highly of a young doctor she knew. Lily was just about finished with school and Junie, the baby, was now fifteen years old. The last time Sadie had seen Junie, the girl had been just a few short months away from her sixth birthday—the same age Sadie had been when she'd become the *de facto* mother of the house.

They all came to visit her in jail. Even Aunt Ethel came, looking older but not exactly old. "Well, you finally got caught," Aunt Ethel sniffed, blotting her eyes with a handkerchief.

"I did." Thus far, her sisters had made no mention of Sadie's disreputable life. But surely Aunt Ethel had realized that a single woman alone in Texas could only earn the amount of money Sadie did one way.

Aunt Ethel looked well—they all had. The Billington women were well fed and well educated. It did Sadie good to see that they had turned out so well. Because of her, her sisters had had a chance to do something with their lives. They were educated. They could choose their future.

They could do what they wanted. And in that, at least, all of the Billington women were alike.

"Do they know what you've done?" Aunt Ethel asked, dropping her voice to a whisper.

Sadie understood the question. "No. May suspects, but I don't think they want to admit it. Not out loud, anyway."

Ethel nodded. Sadie had so few good memories of her mother. The woman had been sickly and abed most of Sadie's life. But Ethel had been Olivia's older sister and Ethel had remained a spinster. Was this what her mother could have been, if she hadn't been burdened with six babies?

"You can't tell them," Ethel finally said, wringing her handkerchief in her hands. "May's going to marry the pastor. A good man, he is, but…"

"But having his future sister-in-law publically acknowledged as a notorious whore would hurt his reputation in the community," Sadie sighed. She wasn't surprised. After all, wasn't that the exact same reason Gerard had disguised his appearance to come visit her in the Jeweled Ladies? "It'll come out in the trial, though."

Ethel was going to destroy that embroidered piece of cloth. "It wouldn't if…"

Everything about Sadie went still. "If?"

Tears began to roll down Ethel's face. "You've given us so much. When I think of what would have happened to all of us without your sacrifices…"

There was a loud pounding in her ears, like someone hitting a pipe with a hammer. "It wasn't a sacrifice," she mumbled. "I wanted to do it. I liked it."

Which was not the whole truth. She'd liked it, but she'd loved being Gerard's. If Jonathan had offered to take her away from the Jeweled Ladies and make her his wife all those years ago, she would have willingly left her life of sin behind.

But she wasn't the kind of woman men married.

Ethel sniffed. Sadie couldn't tell if it was a sniff of sadness or of disgust. "Dear girl…"

She didn't want to hear whatever Ethel was going to say. "You want me to plead guilty."

Her aunt nodded, too torn to even say the word out loud.

In the end, Sadie had always known it would come down to this, hadn't she? She'd done her best to care for her family in her own fashion. But she'd also chased what she wanted. Desire and surrender, she'd wanted more than she would ever have gotten out of the marriage bed. At least she'd gotten paid for it. But her freedom could still cost them theirs. If only there was another way out of this mess. But she didn't know enough of the law to know what that way could possibly be.

That thought filled her with loneliness all over again because Gerard might have been able to see a way out of this that didn't require her to go to prison and also didn't destroy her sisters' chances. But she'd left him in Brimstone and he…

He'd let her go. He hadn't had a choice. She'd broken the law, after all.

Would he miss her? Perhaps that wasn't the right question because she felt sure that he would miss the times when she'd submitted to him. But would he miss *her*—Sadie Billington? Or would he take what she'd taught him and apply it to the world around him? Would he find a woman whose tastes ran toward his own instead of away from him? Would he finally find peace with himself and with the town of Brimstone? She hoped so. And maybe, when she'd served her sentence, she might seek him out again—not for her own desires, but to make sure that he was doing well. Yes. That was all she needed—to know that he was well.

She hadn't been able to be a mother to her sisters and she wouldn't be able to be a respectable wife in polite society. The only thing she could ever hope to accomplish was that she left people better off than they had been. Her sisters were happy and educated. Ethel had made a home for them. Gerard no longer hated himself and his demons.

That was how she was useful. That was the best she could hope for in this life.

"Don't worry," she said, steeling herself for the future. She'd had a good ten years with the freedom to do whatever she wanted. She'd lived independently and comfortably. Most women didn't even get that. Ethel certainly hadn't.

She patted Ethel on the hand. "I'll do what needs to be done. But they must *never* know. Don't bring them to court." She had her pride. She wanted to have her clothes ripped from her body and her back flogged, but she couldn't take the pain of having her sisters see her lowered like that. "Don't let them back in this jail, either."

"They miss you," Ethel said, but she nodded tearfully. "They don't want to lose you again."

Sadie laughed. It came from a place deep inside of her. The laughter shook her so hard that she had trouble standing. She staggered back to sit on her bunk.

"Oh, Ethel," she said, wiping tears from her face as she stared up at the older woman's worried face. "I was lost a long time ago."

She wished to hell that she'd never been found.

*

A week and a half had passed since Gerard had watched Sadie ride down the street and out of Brimstone. It shouldn't have been this hard, being without her. He'd been alone for decades. He should be used to it.

He wasn't.

Finally, he had the last piece he needed. The letter from Titus was safely tucked into his jacket pocket but he kept touching it to make sure it was still there all the same. The location of one Mr. Jack Wyeth and the fact that his income was lean. The man had suffered losses speculating on gold mines. Which was perfect for Gerard's purposes.

Now he just needed to put the rest of his plan in motion and hope to heaven above that he wasn't too late.

He stood on the porch of the Dupree mansion for what felt like hours after he knocked, waiting for someone to answer the door. He didn't want to do this but there was no other option. Not if he wanted Sadie back, her name cleared. When it finally swung open, he couldn't even pretend to be surprised to see Hank O'Shea standing there, his jacket off and his sleeves rolled up. He didn't even have his collar on.

"Judge Hobson. This is unexpected," O'Shea said, his Irish accent burring the words together.

Right. No doubt everyone would've expected hell to freeze over before he voluntarily came to Raymond Dupree for help. "I need to speak with the mayor and Mrs. Dupree." O'Shea notched an eyebrow at him but otherwise didn't move. Gerard gritted his teeth and said, "Please. It's about Miss Billington."

"Wait here." Before Gerard could process the insult, O'Shea had shut the door in his face.

The nerve of leaving him, of all people, standing out on the porch like a deliveryman. It was so tempting to get wrapped up in his anger at Dupree all over again. But he didn't allow that to control him. There were bigger things at stake than his pride, obviously. He wouldn't be here if that weren't the case.

It took real effort to keep his emotions in control, but he was proud of the way he did so. When the door swung open and Raymond Dupree himself stood there, looking more than a little worried, Gerard was confident that he could get through this evening with his dignity intact even if his pride was a total loss. "Good evening, Mayor Dupree. I'd like a word."

There was a cautiousness in Dupree's gaze. Maybe it had always been there. But for the first time, Gerard felt the weight of that hesitation. This was Isabelle's son. "Come in."

He followed Dupree inside. The mayor led him to a formal parlor. Gerard was unsurprised to see O'Shea lurking in the corner of the room while Mrs. Dupree was carefully arranged on a settee in front of the fire. "Mrs. Dupree," Gerard said, bowing toward her. "You're looking well this evening." There. Mistress would be proud of him. Compliments were always good.

O'Shea growled and stepped closer. "Is this some sort of trick, Hobson? Because it takes a lot of nerve to walk in here after what you've done."

The mayor's wife didn't so much as raise a hand toward O'Shea. She merely slid him a look out of the corner of her eye, but the effect was immediate. O'Shea straightened up and closed his mouth.

Gerard took a moment to make sure that he was in command of all his senses. He would not let his darkness win out. "I have come to ask for a favor."

A silence that could only be described as stunned filled the room.

"Jesus," O'Shea muttered.

Dupree moved to stand behind his wife, resting a hand on her shoulder. She reached up and placed her fingers on his, a simple gesture of support and comfort.

"What sort of favor?" Dupree asked.

There is only one way to do this. Directly. "I would like your help in getting a position in Austin."

Dupree, his wife, and O'Shea all shared a glance. But no one laughed and no one cursed. That was probably as good as it was going to get. "Is there a reason?" Dupree asked, ever the politician.

"I would like to resign my position on the bench in Brimstone. I would like to leave this town to you." He could feel the back of his neck burning, but he couldn't stop. This was his only hope. "I find my taste for this town has changed and I think it would be best if I went somewhere else and started over."

Their silence in the face of these statements was unnerving. He was putting himself at their mercies and he did not like it.

"You told Hank... Sadie?" Mrs. Dupree asked in a voice that seemed small.

"Yes." He was doing this wrong, he realized. Mentally, he kicked himself. "Let me begin again. I owe each of you apology." He'd thought the words might be harder to say, but they flowed. He turned to O'Shea. "You have been a worthy opponent. I should

221

not have tried to dig into your past, although you've hid it quite well. I promise that I will not do such a thing again."

Another raised eyebrow. "I'm not the one you need to be apologizing to."

Gerard nodded. Of course the man was right. He turned his attention to Mrs. Dupree. "My dear lady, I have wronged you most terribly. I have impugned upon your honor and for that I offer my deepest apologies."

"I accept your apology," Mrs. Dupree said after a moment's hesitation, "but I wonder at the reason behind it. You will forgive me for saying, but it seems to be a rather sudden change of heart."

"Perhaps not so sudden," Dupree said, studying him carefully. "This is about Sadie, is it not?"

Gerard took a deep breath as he stared at Raymond Dupree. "You look like her. I never..." He found he needed to take another deep breath, but it was harder this time because his chest felt tight. "I never told her that. Although I'm sure she knew."

"I knew it," O'Shea muttered, but Mrs. Dupree silenced him with another cold look.

"Knew what?" Dupree said.

He just had to get this over with and then hope that they would agree to help them. "I was in love with your mother. I asked her to marry me and, to her credit, she refused. She had her reasons." Even though he was essentially confessing, he couldn't bring himself to admit that Isabelle had thought him a monster. "She married your father and had you and I am ashamed to admit that I have spent the better part of the last thirty years trying to punish you because of her choices. I've only recently come to see that we would've made a poor match. I could not have made her happy and I now realize that she could not have made me happy, either."

"I knew it," O'Shea repeated, sounding unnecessarily pleased with himself.

"Why are you admitting this now?" Dupree said, looking pale.

Before Gerard could answer, Mrs. Dupree did it for him. "Because of Sadie."

There was nothing harder than watching Sadie ride away from him. In comparison, making apologies was easy. "Your wife is correct. I know that I condemned you for marrying a..." O'Shea cleared his throat forcefully. "A Jewel," Gerard finished, working mightily to keep his tone level. "I realize that I have campaigned against you based on your morals. So that is why I have hidden my connection with Sadie for months now."

Mrs. Dupree dropped her head, her gaze fastened on her lap.

Dupree said, "You've been patronizing the Jeweled Ladies?" and everything in his tone suggested disbelief and judgment and maybe even a touch of sheer horror. That was why Gerard would have to leave.

In his mind, he'd gone through all of the ways he could explain his relationship with Sadie. None of those explanations seemed to readily volunteer themselves at this time, however. So instead of a rational, logical argument, he said, "Sadie is special. Your wife, no doubt, already knew this. And Mr. O'Shea probably has also made his guesses."

"I knew it." This time, O'Shea didn't even bother to whisper.

"Hush, Hank," Mrs. Dupree hissed. And she turned her attention to Gerard and suddenly, she was the only person in the room who mattered. "She said she could handle you. She said she trusted you not to harm her. And *you* had her arrested. Why should we do a favor for you? Sadie's entire world is based on trust and you violated that rather unforgettably."

Gerard hung his head because she was right. "I want to marry her. But I don't think that I am strong enough to marry her here. Not because I am ashamed of her," he added when Mrs. Dupree gasped. "I would do anything to protect her and I don't think that I could walk down the streets of Brimstone with her on my arm and not want to kill every man who looks at her and sneers. I don't know how you do it, Dupree. Only that you are a better man than I am. I think you always have been."

"You're serious, aren't you? About marrying her?" Dupree stepped around the settee, stopping only a feet away from Gerard. "About killing people who looked at her?"

"Knowing him, he'd only beat them severely," O'Shea muttered.

"Hank," Mrs. Dupree said again, growing more exasperated by the second. "So why are you here, Judge Hobson?"

"My man Titus has found the gentleman that Sadie stole from. I'm leaving for Kentucky in the morning in the hopes that I make it before she does anything foolish like plead guilty," he explained. "I'm going to make complete restitution in her name, try to get the charges dropped and then I'm going to ask her to marry me. And after that, I think we would both enjoy a chance to go somewhere fresh and start our lives anew. To that end," he said, turning his attention back to Dupree, "I've come to ask for a favor. I cannot give up the law. It is too much part of who I am. But Brimstone is no longer my home because Sadie is not here. If you could find a way to recommend me to a position in Austin, continuing to do legal work as befitting someone of my experience, I would be most grateful."

"The nerve," O'Shea muttered again.

"I am *trying* to explain," Gerard snapped. "I would leave Brimstone and I would not come back," he pressed on, determined to control his temper and ignore the Irishman. "For too many years, I allowed a misguided sense of hatred determine my actions. I convinced myself that what I was doing was moral, ethical and legal. I believed that the women of the Jeweled Ladies and the other brothels in this town, as well as all of the people who patronized them, were sinners doomed to burn in hell. I believed that if I could just make everyone follow the rules, this would be a sort of... a utopia."

His words settled around the room, and for once, O'Shea didn't sneer. Gerard pressed on, mindful that time was growing short. He would leave in the morning, but he wanted to know he could provide a future for Sadie. "But I was the one who was wrong. The law is good for many things, but it cannot account for a woman stealing a few hundred dollars to keep her sisters from having to walk the streets. Morality is good, but it cannot account for the way that God has

225

made some people." It was a hedge. He could see it in their faces. So he took a deep breath and tried again. He was done lying to himself. "From the way He has made *me*. My behavior has been anything but ethical toward you. So this is what I ask. Help me leave this town and I will never bother you again. You have been a…" His throat unexpectedly closed up. "A fine mayor and I know that your parents were proud of you and, were they still here, they would continue to be proud of you."

Dupree blinked at him. "Thank you for that."

Gerard was sure that he was imagining any shining in the mayor's eyes. Lord knew his eyes were itching. The smoke from the chimney must have blown back into the room.

"Let me get this straight," O'Shea began. Mrs. Dupree tried to *hush* him again, but he ignored her. "You want us to get you a position in the governor's office or in the statehouse in exchange for promising to leave Brimstone forever?"

"And Sadie," Mrs. Dupree added. "You would marry her, treat her well?"

"I would do anything for her." That was the simple, unvarnished truth. "If I had the means, I would retire entirely. I would never seek office or practice law again. However, I am afraid that it will take most of the rest of my funds to pay back her debt and I would not marry her only to keep her in poverty, so I need to work. But I swear, I would never do anything without her permission."

"I'm not sure I understand what this is about," Dupree said, sitting down next to his wife on the settee.

Gerard's idea of hell would be having to explain what, *exactly*, this was about. It was bad enough that Mrs. Dupree and O'Shea undoubtedly surmised the sort of relationship he had with Sadie. He wasn't sure he could admit it out loud, to Isabelle's son, no less.

Mrs. Dupree patted him on the arm. "It's all right, dear. The important thing is that the judge and Sadie are, in fact, perfectly suited to each other." Her gaze raked over Gerard and in that moment, he saw the woman who at one time was supposed to replace Mistress as the proprietor of the Jeweled Ladies. "And if Sadie refuses you?"

He closed his eyes and breathed in and out. "Then I will have no choice but to honor her wishes. She is the one in control. She has always been so."

"Never thought I'd see the day," O'Shea said, laughing under his breath.

"Oh, Hank," Mrs. Dupree scolded. Then she turned to her husband. "Could you help him?"

Dupree looked shaken. But for that, he didn't look a coward. He instead looked like a man who had to re-examine some closely held beliefs. Gerard sympathized. "If we help you, you will leave."

"Yes. And," he added, sensing that his goal was within his grasp, "I would be in your debt. A position in Austin could have the potential to be to your benefit in the long run."

That wiped the smirk off O'Shea's face. He lifted his eyebrows and leaned forward. "You're serious, aren't you?"

He was tired of talking. He needed to be arranging his affairs, just in case. Everything he had was Sadie's, whether she knew it or not. "Are you

227

going to help me?" He focused his attention on Dupree. He could understand why no one in this room would rush to help him, but surely the mayor could see the wisdom in having an ally at the Statehouse.

Dupree looked at his wife, who gave a little nod of her head. Then he looked at O'Shea, who shrugged. Dupree stood and extended his hand. "I have your word?"

"You do."

They shook on it. The corner of Dupree's mouth curved up into a smile that Gerard recognized as Isabelle's. He was afraid it would hurt more than it did. But it didn't. It just felt like a... Like a memory. One that was ready to be put away. "I think I have a solution."

Good. Gerard was done with memories.

For the first time, he was truly focused on the future.

His future.

Chapter Twenty

She could get through this. That was what Sadie told herself over and over again. She could get through this wait, this trial, this embarrassment, and this sentencing. If anyone could handle being deprived of her freedom for a few years, it would be her.

Because she was going to plead guilty, she hadn't even engaged the services of a lawyer. Lawyers cost money and why waste it? It'd be better spent on Daisy's studies.

Finally, after long, dull weeks, her trial date had arrived. She was led into the courtroom by a bailiff. The handcuffs were heavy on her wrist, but Sadie knew better than to show fear. She may be here to admit to her crime, but she would not admit regret. She was treated differently here than she was in Brimstone. There, she was afforded a measure of respect because she was Sapphire Bleu, one of the Jeweled Ladies. Here, the Billington name got her nothing at all, except sneers of condescension.

Sadie sat with the other criminals and waited for her case to be called. She was off to the side where only a few women were sitting. Most of them appeared to be whores, just like her. Maybe they recognized something in her, because they treated her with civility. Professional courtesy, even.

Time passed slowly as she waited for her case to be called. Finally, the judge read her name. She stood and was led to the front of the room, where the prosecutor, a wiry man with wiry glasses, read the charges.

"Young lady," the judge intoned. He was flabby in the jowls with a hangdog look. Nothing like Gerard. "You've been accused of stealing a great deal of money. Do you have a lawyer to represent you?"

Before Sadie could respond, a door in the back of the courtroom banged open.

"I'm here to represent Miss Billington," a voice announced into the room. That voice commanded authority and respect. That voice carried over the shocked gasps of the gathered crowd. That voice sent a shiver down her back and brought a smile to her face.

He shouldn't be here. He shouldn't have come for her. But he had.

Gerard Hobson was in the room.

She lifted her chin and smiled at the judge on the bench. He scowled at her. "Who are you?"

"Gerard Hobson, Esquire."

A confused hush fell over the courtroom. Sadie schooled her features carefully so that she would not smirk. Of course his name didn't mean anything here in Kentucky. This wasn't Brimstone, after all. It would be informative to see how Gerard handled himself when his reputation did not precede him. But underneath that there was a feeling of warmth and satisfaction. He was here to take care of her. Wasn't that wonderful?

The judge on the bench notched an eyebrow at her, looking bored with this situation. "Is this your lawyer, miss?"

By that time, Gerard had made his way to her side. She looked at him and couldn't fight the smile. He was here.

"Well, Miss Billington?" Gerard said in a voice for her ears only. "Do you consent?"

It couldn't be anything but love, could it? It must've taken him days to get here. It's not like he was in the area and decided to drop by.

He had promised to protect her, to take care of her and he was doing just that.

"I do."

Gerard nodded toward the bench, so Sadie repeated her statement for the benefit of the court.

The judge exhaled heavily and looked at his pocket watch. "Shall we get on with it? How do you plead, Miss Billington?"

Sadie opened her mouth, but Gerard put a hand on her shoulder. "I would like the charges dropped, Your Honor."

"Objection," the prosecutor all but yelped in surprise. He clearly hadn't been expecting anything other than a token resistance.

The judge's jowls shifted as he frowned down at Gerard. "For what reason?"

Gerard looked back into the courtroom and motioned. A man whom Sadie hadn't noticed before came forward. He was heavyset, with a bowler hat crammed down over his head. He seemed vaguely familiar... And then it hit her. This was her former fiancé, the man she'd stolen five hundred dollars from. What was he doing here?

"If it pleases the court, Your Honor, this is Mr. Jack Wyeth. He is the victim in the case." Everything

231

about Gerard spoke to a certainty that he was in the right. It sent another shiver down her back. God, she'd missed him.

Sadie looked at Jack in shock. Had she ever even thought about marrying that man? It wasn't that he looked so much older now. Gerard was older. But what had seemed like wealth and respectability then now looked worn and shabby on him. The years had not treated him kindly and she hoped that was not due directly to her theft.

"Well?" the judge on the bench said. At least he now looked moderately interested in the case. "Speak up, Mr. Wyeth."

"Um, Your Honor? Restitution?" He looked at Gerard. "Was that the right word?"

Sadie smiled. She knew the Gerard was trying to look supportive, but it was not an expression that came naturally to him. Instead, he looked like he was going to bite something. "Yes."

"I've been paid back," Jack announced. Sweat was beading along his neck and he looked horrified to be here. "With interest. I don't wish to press charges."

She'd almost married him? Thank God she'd run. But... Wait. He'd been paid back? Was this even possible? It was too much. Little pops of color went off at the edge of Sadie's vision.

The judge on the bench did not look impressed. He turned to the prosecutor, pocket watch already in hand again. They were wasting time. The thought made her want to laugh again. To the judge and the prosecutor and everyone else in this courtroom, this was another ten minutes taken from their lunch break. To her, it was her life.

232

"Well?" the judge demanded.

The prosecutor was staring at Gerard as if the man had appeared out of a cloud of smoke and made an offer on his eternal soul. "I'm sorry. Who are you, again?"

"Gerard Hobson," he replied, smooth and unruffled. "Special council to Elisha M. Pease."

The pops of color got a little brighter.

"Who?" the prosecutor repeated, dumbfounded. He didn't recognize the name. But Sadie did.

The muscles in Gerard's neck tightened as his entire body coiled with brutal energy. If the prosecutor knew what was good for him, he'd run. The wiry little man had already backed up a step.

"The governor of Texas. Maybe you've heard of that state, sir?" Gerard didn't thunder it. He spoke in a silky voice that was just that menacing. The prosecutor paled. "Or are you so woefully uneducated that you have not yet seen fit to learn about this great union that you are, in theory, representing in court today?" Gerard stared down the prosecutor, who seemed to shrink.

"I—I—" the prosecutor babbled.

Gerard sighed heavily and turned his attention back to the judge, who at least now looked interested. "Your honor, we had hoped to resolve this issue without involving Governor Stevenson. But if the prosecutor is not fit to handle this case…"

Sadie gasped. She had no idea what game Gerard was playing, but this couldn't be true, could it? He wouldn't dare walk into a court of law, even if it was in Kentucky, and tell such a bald-faced lie.

Would he?

233

The judge's mouth opened and closed as he looked helplessly at the prosecutor, who seemed too stunned to do anything but waver where he stood. Dominance radiated off Gerard and Sadie wanted to do nothing more than sink to her knees and lean against him. But she didn't. Right now, he was acting as a member of the court. And she wasn't free yet.

The prosecutor made a show of pulling himself together by straightening his cuffs and smoothing his moustache. "No, no. There's no need to involve our fine governor. Restitution has been made and if the victim is satisfied…"

Everyone turned to Jack Wyeth, who was startled to find himself the center of attention again. "Ah, yes. I'm satisfied."

The prosecutor exhaled heavily. "Fine. Restitution made, charges dropped."

The judge banged his gavel. "Charges dropped. Miss Billington, you're free to go."

Her knees did weaken then, but Gerard's arms encircled her waist and then he was half carrying, half leading her out of the courtroom. Once the doors had swung shut behind them, he picked up her hand and tucked it into the crook of his arm before heading toward the front door of the courthouse.

They stepped outside and the bright sunshine hit her in the face for the first time in weeks. Sadie took a moment to breathe deeply. Kentucky had a smell different from Texas. The air was wetter here and smelled more of green grass than it did in Texas. Texas smelled like wind and dirt and…

And Gerard.

She was walking on Gerard's arm in the light of

day. The charges had been dropped and she no longer needed to worry about her past. The life of Sapphire Bleu had not come to light during the trial. Her sisters were saved. Sadie wasn't a criminal anymore.

And Gerard had come for her.

"How did you do that?" she asked.

He chuckled, a warm sound that surrounded her. "Titus is slow, but he does good work. It took him a little bit longer to find Mr. Wyeth than I would've liked."

"I don't understand. You found Jack and paid him back? For *me*?"

"Well," Gerard said she could hear the humor lacing his voice. "He needed a little convincing. It turns out that being rejected by someone as beautiful as Sadie Billington can scar a man."

She dropped her head. He'd been rejected once. She simply did not care about Jack, but it pained her to think that she might have led to years of suffering on his behalf. "How did you get him to agree?"

Gerard chuckled and she leaned into him. "I paid him a great deal of interest."

Sadie stopped and looked up at him. "*Gerard.*"

"What?" Looking innocent did not come naturally to the man. He couldn't pull it off without smirking.

"Is that even legal?"

His eyes got wider. "Is what legal?"

She glared at him. "Bribing a witness? For heaven's sake, you just walked into a courtroom and threatened to involve two governors! Since when do you work for Governor Pease? I thought you were a judge! In Brimstone!"

235

He looked down at her, warmth in his eyes. "I was. But I'm not anymore."

The pops of color were back. "You quit the bench? But you love your work!"

It wasn't decent, the way he cupped her cheek in the palm of his hand in broad daylight, in the middle of the street, with people milling all around them. It wasn't decent, the way he leaned down and kissed her—her!—in front of God and man. And it certainly wasn't decent the way he whispered against her lips, "I found something that I love more than the law."

Chapter Twenty-One

Sadie's eyes rolled back into her head. Gerard barely had time to sweep her up into his arms before she went completely limp. Good lord, she'd fainted. For a moment, he was paralyzed with fear. What was he supposed to do with her now?

Take care of her.

What he needed was a carriage. It wasn't easy to wave one down with her warm weight in his arms but he managed. In short order, he had her inside and had given instructions to the driver. Then he climbed in after her and pulled her into his lap.

"My love," he murmured. "Are you all right?"

"Gerard…" her voice was faint against his cheek, but then her arms came up around his neck and his Sadie was back in his arms again.

"*Shh,*" he whispered, stroking her hair. "It's all right, pet. I promised to take care of you and so I shall. I can only hope you'll forgive me for not getting to you sooner."

"I can't," she replied, trying to push back. But the carriage jerked and he had no choice but to fold his arms around her again. "This isn't right, Gerard. You can't give up your career for me. I'm not—" She choked on a sob. "I'm not worth it."

His grip on her tightened. "What?"

"I'm not the kind of woman men marry." Her voice had gotten small again. He did not like it.

"Who said that to you?"

She didn't reply. Not in words. Instead, she curled up into his lap, small and vulnerable. He wanted to order her to tell him, but this was not the game. This was their lives. And he could not expect total honesty from her if he did not offer it himself.

"The woman who rejected me? Who called me a monster and then married another? That was Raymond Dupree's mother."

She jolted so hard in his lap that she almost fell to the floor. "What?"

"I didn't want to admit, even to you, that the reason I have been stuck in this feud with the mayor is because he was..." Gerard sighed, tucking Sadie into his arms. "He represented my failure. He was the son I should have had."

"I... I should have known." She relaxed against him and her arms went around his neck.

"Very few people do. So, now you know the whole story. Will you not tell me yours? Because I happen to think you are exactly the kind of woman I should marry."

They rode on in silence for a while, but he did not push her. She'd been through a great deal today and perhaps it was unfair to ask this of her.

"His name was Jonathan," she finally said in a voice so quiet he had to bend his head to catch it. Hearing another man's name on her lips knotted up his gut, but he forced himself to be calm, for her sake. "He came to the Jeweled Ladies for a few months. He was a master and I made the foolish mistake of confusing acceptance with affection."

"Ah. So that is why you warned me." She nodded against his neck. "What happened?" He steeled himself for the rest of this story. He wasn't going to like it because someone had hurt his Sadie. But then, she hadn't been his at the time, so he had no quarter to speak.

"I would have gone anywhere with him, done anything for him. I fancied myself in love. Then one day he showed up with a necklace and said he was leaving. He'd found a proper woman to marry him and I…" her voice trailed off.

Gerard focused on breathing steadily. He would not track down this Jonathan and challenge him. He would not avenge Sadie's hurt. He could not change her past any more than he could change his own. But it still hurt him to know that she was scarred by this man she'd given herself to so completely. "You asked him to take you with him?"

"I did. I was pitiful. And he said…" She swallowed again as he felt damp tears against his skin. "That women like me were not for marrying."

"He was wrong," Gerard said fiercely. "He was very, very wrong. My dear girl, you told me once that it was a good thing that Isabelle did not marry me because we both would have been miserable, did you not?"

She nodded again, her chest hitching up.

"No doubt he is just as miserable, do you not think? You could have made him happy and he put his reputation above that."

"I don't want children," she whispered. "I raised

my sisters, but Jack, Mr. Wyeth, he wanted a big
family and I couldn't do it."

Gerard couldn't help himself. He kissed her then
and slid his hand up under her skirts. When she
gasped, he sank his fingers into her hair and tilted her
head back until she had no choice but to look him in
the eyes.

"My love, I am an old man. Far too old for you,"
he added, tightening his grip on her tresses. "What
would I do with children? Spend the rest of my life
explaining they were my own, not my grandchildren? I
have not a paternal bone in my body, and besides, I am
too selfish. I would marry you and keep you all to
myself. If you would have me." It was not the most
gracious of proposals.

Her eyes began to water again and he released his
grip on her hair. But that did not stop her tears. "Do
you mean it, Gerard?"

"I gave up my position for you. I am giving up
Brimstone for you. The mayor generously consented
to recommend me for a position in the Governor's
office, providing legal counsel. I will be moving to
Austin as soon as we get back to Texas. It would make
me happy if you joined me there as my bride, Sadie."

She was going to say yes. He could see it in her
smile, her happy tears. But then that light dimmed.
"I'm nothing but a criminal and a prostitute."

He appeared to think this over. "Correction.
Sapphire Bleu was prostitute. Sadie Billington was
involved in a... misunderstanding, shall we say, and
had the charges dropped and therefore is *not* a
criminal." He shifted, letting her weight grind against
his growing erection. "Sadie Hobson, however, would

be a polite, respectable young bride." She gasped and his grin turned wicked. "In public, anyway."

Her eyes fluttered again and he feared she was on the verge of fainting again.

"Why are you here?" she asked. But this time, instead of weakness or vulnerability in her voice, he heard strength. She was the strongest woman he'd ever known.

"Because I choose to be here. I choose you, Sadie. I will always choose you. I can only hope that you'll consent to choose me, too." Then he waited for her answer.

The carriage rattled down the streets of Lexington for the longest moments in his life. If she said no, he had to respect that. He could not impose his will on her, any more than he could impose his will upon the people of Brimstone.

Then she leaned back and looked him in the eyes, her face bright and her smile happy, and a great weight lifted off Gerard's chest. "I choose to go wherever you go, Gerard. I will gladly be your wife."

He crushed her into a great hug and realized he was laughing and she was laughing and that *this* was happiness.

It was some time later when she pulled away from his kisses to ask, "Um, where are we going?"

"To your aunt's house. I believe I can have a preacher there within an hour—two at the most. I would think you'd like to get married with your sisters as witnesses."

"Oh, Gerard." Her eyes grew wet again.

"And then," he added, feeling wicked again, "I have a room in a fine hotel, just for you and me. Let

241

me take care of you, pet," he murmured, mussing up her hair again. "For the rest of our lives. Do you consent?"

She drew him back into her embrace, strong and vulnerable. He couldn't wait to strip that dress from her body and give her everything she'd ever wanted, everything he'd ever dreamed of. "I do."

About the Author

Thanks so much for reading this *Jeweled Ladies* story! Leaving an honest review or telling a friend what you thought is the best way to show the love for your friendly local author!

Who is Maggie Chase? Writer, reader, crafter—I've told a lot of different stories a lot of different ways as Sarah M. Anderson, but the Jeweled Ladies series marks my first foray into historical erotica. I passionately believe that every single person deserves their own happily-ever-after and my stories reflect that hope on the page.

Readers can find out more about Maggie any of the following ways:

Sign up for her newsletter:
http://bit.ly/maggiechasenews

Visit her website:
http://www.maggiechase.com

Check out her Tumblr:
http://themaggiechase.tumblr.com/

243

Follow on Twitter:
http://twitter.com/TheMaggieChase

Leave a review on Goodreads:
http://www.goodreads.com/maggie_chase

Get Amazon pre-order information:
www.amazon.com/author/maggiechase

Other Books by Maggie Chase

The Jeweled Ladies: The Mistress Series

His Topaz
Their Emerald
Her Ebony
His Sapphire
His Crown Jewel

The Jeweled Ladies: The Rogues Series

His Diamond
His Amethyst

Now Available from Maggie Chase

The Mistress of the Jeweled Ladies keeps her past buried. But when Free Cyrus Franklin walks back into her life, will she be able to put Mistress away and be his Emily again?

Read on for an excerpt of
HIS CROWN JEWEL
a Jeweled Ladies story

Free Cyrus Franklin sat at the scarred table wedged into his tiny kitchen, staring in shock at the note Isaac had just handed him. He looked up at the silent giant of a man. "Is this true?"

Isaac shrugged. Cyrus had a feeling that the man actually could talk—he just chose not to. His reasons were his own.

"And the letter was just delivered?"

Isaac nodded.

Just to be sure, Cyrus read it a third time.

Mistress bought a girl. Young. She's keeping her at the Jeweled Ladies.

The note wasn't signed.

There had to be a mistake. The woman that the rest of Brimstone knew as Mistress would never buy

245

another person. She especially would not buy a little girl. It went against everything she'd ever believed.

At least, it went against everything Emily Weatherspoon believed. But then again, Cyrus didn't know her as well as he once had. He never would've figured she'd have wound up as a madam of a brothel. She'd married a preacher, for God's sake.

Emily Weatherspoon had been the staunchest of abolitionists, a loud voice in the middle of the deep South, pushing not just for slaves' rights, not just for colored rights, but also for women's rights. Even Indian rights. Everyone was equal in her eyes. And more than anything, the girl that Cyrus had known abhorred slavery.

He read the note again.

What he needed was more information. There had to be something else in play here. Cyrus couldn't countenance how running a whorehouse had changed Emily over the years. But he couldn't imagine her sinking to this level. She didn't need the money.

Desperately, he wanted to believe that this was an act of goodness and not one of depravity. The Emily he knew would take a girl in and clothe and feed her. The Emily he knew would protect a child from...

Well, from the likes of Mistress, the most famous whore in Texas.

It hurt his heart to think that this could be anything other than a misunderstanding. Mistress was not the same woman he'd known. She refused to give up that brothel of hers. She refused to stop selling girls to men, one hour at a time. She refused to follow the path of righteous honor that she had always insisted she would.

Another thought occurred to him. What if this wasn't just a sign of her slipping further into depravity? What if this was a sign that she was in trouble in some other way? He knew that she was safe in that house of hers—but he worried. He had no right, but he worried anyway.

Emily Weatherspoon had made it clear that she was not Cyrus's concern and he was not hers.

Which was all well and good to say, but that didn't make it any less true. No matter how much time had passed or how many miles they'd traveled, he and Emily always seemed to come back to one another.

Just like it did every time he thought of her, Cyrus's body tightened. As Mistress, Emily was one of the finest ladies in town, maybe the state. The clothes she wore put her body to its best advantage. It wasn't the body Cyrus remembered, but it was an amazing body. She made those clothes and jewels look so damn good.

More than once, he'd saddled his horse and stowed some money in a saddlebag, intent on riding to town and buying an hour—or a night—of her time. Maybe he'd lay her out on her fine bed and plunge his body into hers over and over again until they were both spent and sated. Then he'd take her again—this time, with her on top, riding him wildly, those beautiful breasts of hers freed from their silk trappings for him to touch and suck and bite.

God, there were so many ways he wanted her. She'd been his every fantasy since he'd been old enough to imagine the sexual act as something to enjoy with another person and every day that slipped past with them not talking, not even acknowledging each other, was another day those fantasies burned in a bonfire of frustration.

Those were the bad nights, the ones where his whole body was an instrument of torture that would never seem to end. Taking himself in hand didn't do much but edge the pain back to manageable levels. On the better nights, he saddled up with better intent. He'd walk into the Jeweled Ladies and pay his money to get her alone and then they'd... they'd talk. They used to talk all the time, when he could slip away from his chores. About nothing and everything. First she'd taught him to read and then she'd snuck him books—books she'd already read, so they could debate the finer points of *Ivanhoe* or Shakespeare or the Bible. He'd give anything to just sit next to her, his arm around her shoulder, and have her talk to him like she used to. Had she read Dickens? He thought she'd like Dickens. Or Scott. Or...

Or anything, as long as they talked. As long as he knew she remembered him.

Either way, with coin in hand, she wouldn't be able to refuse him, would she?

But that was the thought that always stopped him cold. He loved her, he lusted after her, he worried about her—but he wouldn't take her if she couldn't refuse him.

And thus far, she had refused him completely. The last time he'd seen her across the street, she hadn't even smiled at him. It was almost as if he hadn't been there.

He rubbed his palm over the center of his chest and looked up at Isaac, trying to see what he was missing. "That woman who came through a few days ago—she had a lot of money."

Isaac nodded.

"You think she sold the girl?"

Don't miss
HIS CROWN JEWEL
By Maggie Chase
© 2017 by Maggie Chase
Sign up for the Newsletter
Check out www.maggiechase.com
for more great Jeweled Ladies stories!

www.ingramcontent.com/pod-product-compliance
Lightning Source LLC
Chambersburg PA
CBHW020319200626
46814CB00006BA/2323